VIVIENNE

Also by Emmalea Russo

Magenta
Confetti
Wave Archive
G

VIVIENNE

a novel

EMMALEA RUSSO

Arcade Publishing • New York

Arcade Publishing books may be purchased in bulk at special discounts for sales promotion, corporate gifts, fund-raising, or educational purposes. Special editions can also be created to specifications. For details, contact the Special Sales Department, Arcade Publishing, 307 West 36th Street, 11th Floor, New York, NY 10018 or arcade@skyhorsepublishing.com.

Arcade Publishing® is a registered trademark of Skyhorse Publishing, Inc.®, a Delaware corporation.

Visit our website at www.arcadepub.com.
Please follow our publisher Tony Lyons on Instagram @tonylyonsisuncertain

10 9 8 7 6 5 4 3 2 1

Library of Congress Cataloging-in-Publication Data is available on file.

Jacket design by Brian Peterson
Cover image *Faithful Gelert*, engraving by William Henry Mote
from a painting by Daniel Maclise

Print ISBN: 978-1-64821-064-8
Ebook ISBN: 978-1-64821-065-5

Printed in the United States of America

for my father

Insanity is a necessarily occurring form or stage
in the development of the soul.

—Hegel, *Philosophy of Spirit*

CONTENTS

REMOVAL

MAUD
@Maudlin005

Disturbed to hear that @NATMUSEUM is including the harmful
work of Vivienne Volker in their upcoming group show of
Forgotten Surrealist Women
6:00am   December 12
21 shares   **553** likes

@lanced80
VV made torture DRAWINGS
and clothes for tortured DOLLS

@nicoredhead
huh

@lalafigueroa
girls impaled by sewing needles
mutilated dresses
etc

@ermine
in the 70s, Volker sewed a wardrobe
for Hans Bellmer's doll sculptures from the 1930s

@nicoredhead
terror aesthetics

@mickeyroar
Volker is criminal
her 'art' is just the tip
of a fuckt surrealist iceberg

@ermine
what r her crimes

4

Elisa
@Elissssa

My ex told me that Vivienne Volker INCITED Wilma Lang to jump
from Hans Bellmer's window to her death. WHAT R U GOING TO
DO @NATMUSEUM?!
6:55am   December 12
207 shares   **2,498** likes

MAUD
@Maudlin005

vivienne volker killed wilma lang
6:57am   December 12
347 shares   **4,509** likes

@salobay
@NATMUSEUM address this
WHAT THE FUCK?

@ermine
chill
lang died by suicide, 1970s

@fdah
POV: yr in a group show with yr murderer

@lalafigueroa
can't get murdered 2x

@ermine
has the artist commented?

@nellyr
vv doesn't speak
about her work

@mickeyroar
does she speak abt her crimes?

@paulinez
WHO IS VIVIENNE VOLKER

@mickeyroar
vile artist

@fdah
y include an alleged murderess maker of torture porn
when there is so much GOOD underrepresented work out there

@nellyr
she dserves late career comeback

@paulinez
YALL R PSYCHOZ

@salobay
she pushed a brilliant artist out of window
@NATMUSEUM DO NOT PLATFORM

@nellyr
this wuz what 50 yrs ago

@ermine
sux cause all other FORGOTTEN WOMEN SURREALISTS in
the show are dead like how wld they feel about their work being
shown alongside VVz

@nellyr
who are we to say they DEAD

@ermine
we are living

@lit7703
I ran into Volker in 1989 on a Hollywood street. It was a windy
day. She was wearing a silk bustle and she looked like something
out of a film. The fabric caught on my watch. We locked eyes
while I was trying to unhook us and she told me to be careful.
Then, I realized who she was. I told her I was an admirer and
asked if she was working on anything at the moment. She simply
replied, "Never again."

@user6652001

what did Volker DO after her disappearance in 1977

@89vvc

she just . . . . . . .stopped

i think meb found G-O-D

@systemprocessings

fake woman

@stalled6

Everyone knew Wilma was suicidal after Hans ended their decades-long relationship. It was obvious Hans and Vivienne were seeing each other, and that Vivienne's youth added to her distress.

@systemprocessings

youth in itself a kind of violence

@reactoronica

but now shes a HAG

gahahahah

OPEN LETTER CONCERNING
THE WORK AND LIFE OF VIVIENNE VOLKER

December 15

To All Who Stand For What Is Just:

We, the undersigned, object to Vivienne Volker's work being given a platform at the NAT Museum. While we do not deny the importance of Volker's artistic experiments during a particular time, we are no longer in that time. Much has changed, and we strongly believe that showing the (harmful) work of Volker would be a step in the wrong direction. In addition to the horrific accusations (this is not the first time such concerns have been raised) surrounding her involvement in the death of Wilma Lang, Volker is a dubious figure on other fronts. We, the Coalition for Artistic Harm Reduction (CAHR) have taken the time to analyze Vivienne Volker's *Dressing the Dolls* sculptures alongside what we know of her biography and have concluded that the woman and the work provoke (at least) the following triggers:

Abortion

Amputation

Anxiety

Animal abuse

Attempted murder

Bestiality

Bones

Incest

Pedophilia

Sexual Abuse

Torture

Transmisia

Violence

Additionally, we seek to make the public aware that while Volker's artwork is set to be on display at a prominent, progressive institution this spring, she has renounced the making of art in her private life and has not, to the best of our knowledge, contributed anything to the field in over forty years. This kind of incongruity should sound alarm bells. We ask that the NAT Museum reconsider their decision to show Vivienne Volker's sculptures.

In Solidarity,

Coalition for Artistic Harm Reduction (CAHR)

@poelima
is she wearing a literal trash bag in this photo?

@stalled6
One rainy morning in 1976, Vivienne was waiting for a train with her baby. She stood close to me on the track as we waited for the same train to take us away. She flashed me a mischievous grin. Dumbfounded, I thought of telling her I was a fan, but I looked down at the platform instead. She was wearing the strangest boots and a coat she'd fashioned from (yes, indeed) a black trash bag. She looked so tired and had an odd, memorable energy. My eyes moved from her eyes to her boots, back and forth until the train came and blew the trash bag up.

@poelima
elegant yet brutal
cant buy style like this
i want that bag

@gorpkore
she look like shit
murderess

VIVIENNE VOLKER'S *DRESSING THE DOLLS* SCULPTURES
REMOVED FROM NAT MUSEUM'S SPRING SHOW

December 16

From the NAT Museum's statement: "Due to concerns about the potentially harmful nature of Volker's work, along with serious allegations involving the artist's past, namely her involvement in the suicide of Wilma Lang, a fellow artist whose work is also included in our upcoming show, we are redacting Vivienne Volker's work from *Forgotten Women Surrealists*. However, this is not an act of censorship. At the NAT Museum, we seek to foster artistic freedom in an atmosphere of safety. Wherever possible, we seek to reduce art-induced distress. When we reached out to Ms. Volker for answers, we received no clarification. Due to the severity of the allegations surrounding Volker's personal history alongside the number of disturbances expressed around the violent nature of her work, we have made the difficult decision to remove Volker's *Dressing the Dolls* sculptures from the show. *Forgotten Women Surrealists* will be on view from March 22nd through June 24th. Best wishes for a happy new year. We hope to see you at the museum."

@stalled6
There is simply no way to know.
Maybe Vivienne offered encouragement.
This rumor has circulated on and off for decades.
It's possible Lang asked for help.
I myself would consider assisted suicide.

@frockconsciousva
perhaps Vivienne could help you

@gorpkore
better a friend than the state

@emilywuttt
stylish . . .but borrrrrrrring
RIP

@obitchuary
hi @stalled6: YOU OK?

@lbnfdvxx6
THIS BITCH IS STILL VERY MUCH ALIVE
LIVING IN BUMFUCK, USA
PROB STILL WEARING THAT JANKY COAT

@stalled6
Yes, she is absolutely still alive.
Thank you @obitchuary yes I'm okay
Some relationship troubles
that I won't get into here.

@fornicationstationma
I saw her at a fashion show in Paris held in a circus tent in a far off arrondissement. She looked healthy and happy, but messy and weird, smeared makeup. When the fashion show started, circus music began playing and Vivienne sobbed. Why disavow her of one last hoorah after years of flying under the radar?

@bvv50ssx
so she cried at a fashion show
what does that prove

@veronique
this woman is dead, no?

@stalled6
No, @veronique Vivienne Volker is living.
Wilma Lang, Hans Bellmer's lover of many years
and a fascinating artist
died by suicide (jumped out window)
fifty years ago.

@stuartx
history's trash bin

@obitchuary
there are AT LEAST two worlds
KEEP UP

@stalled6
so many memories

VELOUR, VESTA, & VIVIENNE

VELOUR BELLMER

December 12

6:00 a.m.

LOST DOG. DO NOT CHASE! reads the sign tacked to the tree at the far edge of Velour Bellmer's yard. The dog is called Pepper, a name Velour finds predictably ridiculous, partly because she knows the owner, Lisa, a shrieky woman with fake nails and a mild speed habit. The dog, a tiny yappy thing who resembles Lisa, has been missing for a few days, and as Velour sits at the kitchen table over a coffee with cream and sugar, she glares at the sign while stirring, the gone dog's face glowing beneath streetlight as the hot liquid spins.

The house, a white saltbox, looks miniature in the shade of the gargantuan trees stippling the vast, flat yard which spreads then dissolves into a cornfield. Velour's home sits alone and its insides are larger and more elaborate than you'd think: labyrinthine and sticky, lined with surreal wallpaper that Velour made and applied herself several years ago, a damask pattern of brown, black, and dark purple with occasional white eyeballs shot through with red.

Today, the house's eggshell facade is outshone by the bright white snow falling in large chunks, then clasping green-black grass. Velour likes to wake at least an hour before the sun. When everyone's asleep, she can stare into inky space. Velour's husband, an artist-slash-restaurant manager, overdosed on heroin three years ago at the shiny white kitchen table she's sitting at now. Vesta, her seven-year-old, wakes at seven and bolts downstairs with the dog. Velour's eighty-two-year-old mother, Vivienne arrives in the kitchen soon after, brooding, chatting, reaching for the cigs. Velour is not the first one up. Lou, Vivienne's forty-year-old boyfriend, has already left for work.

Velour is sure that fate or God—someone, something—is playing sick cosmic tricks on her. Her young daughter is becoming more like her mother each day: alarmingly charming, moody, and suddenly cruel, with capable technician hands and a bonkers artist heart. Velour exhales, trancing into the field. Yes, there are simply too many beings living in her house. Her gaze wanders again toward the image of the skinny chihuahua. Stolen or roadkill by now, she thinks.

As the matte and wide winter sky brightens, Velour pours two splashes of whiskey into her coffee, opens her laptop, and looks over her notes from yesterday. *Fuck,* she mutters, lighting another cigarette and leaning back. Outside, the snow slows. If you were to look in the kitchen window from the LOST DOG sign, Velour's body would be a small white mass, crumpled and twitchy over the table. Three pre-dawn deer in the field and a red-tailed hawk overhead circling.

Velour yearns to be as empty and gone as the edge of the yard the moment it gets eaten by the meadow. There are zero signs of the impending holiday. She has not decorated and the multicolored Christmas lights of town are not visible from here.

Velour's days have been monotone since her husband's overdose. Write, research, clean, chat with her mother and Vesta, rinse and repeat. The quietude is new. Velour's childhood felt like a fast car outgunning something amorphous and many-eyed. Her twenties are a blur of New York City parties and flashes of light accompanied by spurts of insight.

When Velour met Max Furio, this raucous uncertainty continued, as she spent a large portion of her days worrying she'd find him dead. When she finally *did*, a humming possibility fulfilled, everything went snow-mute and dumb. She started to write poems, sketch, and drink—not much— just enough to stay tilted, off kilter, warm. She upped, too, the time she spent researching the work and lives of her father, Hans Bellmer, who died before she was born, and her mother, Vivienne Volker, Hans's final lover.

The first serious change since Max's death occurred back in July when Vivienne received word that her work would appear in the NAT Museum's swanky exhibition of forgotten female Surrealists. Vivienne would be the only living artist in the show, which she saw as an ominous honor. Her mother sets the tone. Velour knows. Vortex-like, everyone's moods get sucked into hers and spat back out, Vivienne-hued. And after the news, she began to think again of her old life, the manic madness of those days in Paris. That's how Vivienne refers to her past—*those days in Paris*. Suddenly, Velour's world was infiltrated, too—*those days in Paris. Those days, those days.* Vivienne regaled the household with stories of making clothes for disturbing dolls out of trash and scraps. She relayed how she conceived her artworks, and at the dinner table one night, told everyone how she conceived Velour, too:

> *Born in France in 1975, Velour was conceived mystically! I swear. Her obsession with endings, finalities, fatalities so obviously corresponds to the fact that it was her father's final secretion that made her. Back then, everything felt fatal, dreamlike, and automatic. I was mad . . . a little . . . sure.*

She even began to spontaneously speak French and doubled (at least) her time at church. Since Vivienne's rediscovery, Vesta has been more deranged than usual, too. Running manically around with the dog, she takes things apart (board games, for instance) and tapes the pieces to her walls, attempts to shove her fallen baby teeth back up into her gums, on and on. When the school called in September asking if perhaps Vesta needed ADHD meds, Vivienne screamed *CHILD POISONERS!* before abruptly hanging up, she and Lou laughing hysterically while galloping up the spiral staircase. Yes, Vivienne's impending comeback had certainly electrocuted this home and its sinuous residents. Velour feels herself to be the only normal one.

This morning, staring into her coffee as it stops spinning, Velour feels that things are about to shift, again. She can almost—almost—almost—see the end.

~

She takes a sip of coffee then ashes into the giant ashtray at the center of the table, a gift from the painter Dorothea Tanning before her death. It features a miniature version of Tanning's 1943 painting *Eine Kleine Nachtmusik*, in which two little girl automatons sleepwalk through a long hotel hallway. One of the girls has gravity-defying hair pointed up to the ceiling as though electroshocked by air, and both wear skirts of rough white water, a tentacular sunflower attached to one of their oceanic outfits. She stubs her cigarette out on one of the little girls and looks for a long while at its ember-covered head.

Vesta's staccato footsteps shake the whole place, declaring that she's awake. Velour wraps her white robe in anticipation (her mother made it from the material that is her namesake) tighter and tighter around her body, tying a knot while muttering *fuck*. It's Sunday and Vesta and the sun are already up, but she'd needed to get more writing and research done, needed to empty more of her head before it gets filled by mind-numbing tasks which daily present themselves. One by one: never-ending, relentless, comforting, dizzying. She can already see the day's remains circling the drain.

Velour nods to the dog, Franz Kline, a big brindled mutt who sleeps with Vesta. Though only five-years old, Franz, found in a cardboard box outside the grocery store by Max Furio, has an ancient air which disturbs

Velour, who has never been an animal person. It was Franz Kline who found Max at the kitchen table and it was Franz Kline who then nudged Velour awake on that Saturday morning in mid-December as autumn crawled toward its official end. Since Max's death, Vesta and the dog have been inseparable. At seventy-odd pounds, the dog weighs more than the girl.

-Morning, Vest.

-I want waffles!

-You can make them yourself.

-Franz *baby*, are you hungry? Vesta sing-songs.

-*You* feed him, okay? I've already had a long and unproductive day.

Vesta raises an eyebrow, then fills Franz's dish with dry food before popping two frozen waffles into the toaster, humming.

-Did they find Pepper? Vesta asks.

-Doubt it.

-I dreamed of her, the girl says.

-What happened?

Vesta mimes hanging herself, tongue out, as Franz scarfs his food down. Velour cringes at the slurping and chewing sounds.

-You dreamed the dog *killed herself*?

Vesta nods, still cheery.

-Dogs don't do that.

-How do *you know*?

-They wouldn't think to.

-Why?

-They want to live. They don't have that . . . mechanism. A death drive or whatever.

-Do we have that *mechanism*?

-Yes, Velour says, sighing.

Vesta gazes up at the ceiling, considering this.

Franz sprints across the kitchen and knocks Vesta over. She laughs and opens the door, watching as the dog runs and rolls in the snow. The waffles pop up. Franz shits. Vesta, a steaming waffle in each little hand, sashays to the window then back to her mother. Her chin coming to rest on Velour's bony shoulder.

-I *hate* when you ash on them, the girl says, chewing in her mother's ear.

-That's what they're there for.

-*Doubt it.*

Velour pauses, struck by the freaky accuracy with which her daughter mimics her, like she's listening to her own voice played back. *Doubt it. Doubt it.*

-Why is it called an *ash*tray then? Velour asks.

Vesta shrugs, folds a waffle and shoves it into her mouth, then opens the door.

Velour rubs her head as Franz runs into Vesta again. The child shrieks and laughs. Girl and dog race around the kitchen.

-You'll wake Nana, Velour whispers.

She stops, throwing her arms around Franz.

-If dogs can hug, why can't they do suicide?

Stricken with a sense of impending doom, Velour's head pulses with the pain of anticipation. *The end.* The end of what? She's not sure. Of *thought*? Of this particular chapter? Of her mother hovering over their lives like a dark angel? She feels the end approaching but cannot see its contents. So, she focuses on the space where the yard vanishes. A line of snow. Footprints. The rotten, dreary sun. *Fucked.*

-It's just a dream, Velour says.

-Maybe what Dad did was a dream.

Velour lights another cigarette and Vesta scrunches her face.

-Mackenzie's mom said you should *vape.*

-Lisa needs to mind her business. And *please, little miss gossip,* don't go back to Mackenzie and say *la la la my mother said your mother needs to mind her business.*

Vesta giggles.

-And no, what Dad did was *real.* You know that.

Velour realizes she's gripping her robe as she looks at her daughter's pale face, puckered and gathered into the center as if being pulled tight by invisible drawstrings.

-I'm *sad* now, Vesta whispers as she grimly gnaws on the last spongy piece of waffle.

-Well, it's sad, Velour says, smiling, but we can still have a good day.

-That depresses me, Vesta groans.

-*What* depresses you?

-When you *fake it.*

They look out the window. Vesta sits on the black and white kitchen tiles, embracing Franz as he licks the floor.

-Stop! Velour snaps. Vesta's chewing and the dog's tongue are so *loud,* each piece of audio in the room on blast. Vesta scowls at Velour and Velour squints into the field through a cloud of smoke.

-I've just got a bad feeling, Vesta says.

-Everything's fine, Velour says.

Vivienne appears at the entrance to the kitchen like an apparition, calling Velour back into the room. She wears her standard cold weather look: a thick black coat dress which falls almost to the floor. It has puff sleeves and custom buttons by Vivienne. Her hair, streaked white and gray, is gathered into a messy nest at her crown.

Vesta and Franz run to Vivienne's feet, sycophantic.

-I had a *terrible* dream, Vivienne declares, sitting down at the table.

-Me too! Vesta yells.

-What was yours, *mon cherie?*

-A dog hanging from a tree.

-Like in that movie.

-What movie? Velour asks.

-The one Nana showed me.

-Which one?

-*The Passion of Anna,* Vivienne says.

-Mother, why are you showing her Bergman? She's seven.

-Why not?

-I liked it, Vesta reassures.

-You *liked* Bergman? Velour says.

-Uh huh.

-It's so morbid, Velour says to her mother.

Vivienne shrugs, lighting a cigarette.

-What's *morbid*?

-Very interested in death, sad and dark stuff, Velour says, exhaling.

-*You're* morbid, the child replies.

-Nope.

-Well, in case anyone's wondering, I don't remember my dream, Vivienne declares, but I woke up inside a gruesome psychic residue. So I just *knew*.

Velour rolls her eyes. Vesta blinks up at her grandmother, transfixed.

-I have residue, too, says the girl.

-In the movie, the man *rescues* that dog, remember? Vivienne says.

-Yeah! Vesta exclaims.

-How's your tooth? Vivienne asks.

She opens her mouth and reveals a loose tooth. She wiggles it, her eyes filling with tears.

-Does it hurt? Vivienne asks, stroking her granddaughter's cheek.

-No. I just want them to stay *in*, she says, pushing the loose tooth up and into her gum, *I'm gonna kill myself.*

Vivienne cackles.

-Think how stupid it would be to kill yourself over teeth, Vivienne says. Think about that. What are you going to do when you get your *period*?

Vesta presses her finger into her gums and shows Velour a red spot of blood as her scowl morphs into a smile—her expressions so fluid, mutable. She disappears into the living room and when she reemerges, she's wearing her blue winter boots and the black coat her grandmother made for her, essentially the same one Vivienne wears daily, only in miniature, and with puffier sleeves and hot pink buttons, per Vesta's request. Velour thinks her daughter looks like a pale ghost of the gilded age.

-I'm taking Franz on a walk, Vesta says.

-Be careful, says Velour.

~

Vivienne pours coffee into a black teacup and sits beside her daughter at the kitchen table, running her hand over the porcelain surface. She puts her hand on her daughter's hand, a rare instance of physical affection which startles Velour, and says *I'm so happy. I'm old and happy right now at this moment. Want to read me some of your poems?* Velour shakes her head as Vivienne lights a clove. Velour likes her best when not speaking.

-*Be careful, be careful*, Vivienne shakes her head, repeating Velour's warning.

-What?

-Kids are much too protected now. Let her *be*.

-*Let her be*? Let her galavant around town by herself and watch Bergman movies all day?

-Ingmar's movies increase her attention span. Their worst crime is that they are *almost* as boring as the man. Though I only met him the once.

-You're deluded if you think Vesta is too protected. Her father died and she lives with a maniac.

-Don't talk about yourself that way, Vivienne smirks. They throw their heads back in tandem. Laughter.

-Just be glad that girl *has* a spark. She's no *automaton*.

-And I am?

-I didn't say that.

The women sit in silence as Vivienne nibbles on bird-sized bites of waffle, letting the tiny pieces drown in syrup. Velour rubs her head and stares into the amber puddles, disgusted.

~

Halfway through Velour's fourth smoke of the morning, she receives a text message from Clorinda Salazar, an old friend from her time in New York. Clorinda partied with Velour and Max before they moved to the country. They stumbled upon the old home outside a small town in south-eastern Pennsylvania while aimlessly driving. It was *fate*. That's what Max called it, anyway. They spent the next several years fixing it up, retreating from the scene. She thinks of those days often—of happening upon the rundown, two-hundred-year-old house, how the hills were green and brown and blue somehow, the distance spreading into textured checkers. Velour doesn't make an effort to keep in touch with anyone from the past. Clorinda, however, occasionally sends updates and gossip. Though, in recent years, the updates had become rarer.

CLORINDA SALAZAR 7:27am
Your Mom is going viral:

> **Elisa**
> **@Elissssa**
>
> My ex told me that Vivienne Volker INCITED Wilma Lang to jump from Hans Bellmer's window to her death. WHAT R U GOING TO DO @NATMUSEUM?!
> 6:55am   December 12
> **201** shares   **2,498** likes

> **MAUD**
> **@Maudlin005**
>
> vivienne volker killed wilma lang
> 6:57am   December 12
> **347** shares   **4,509** likes

-What's wrong? Vivienne asks.

-Nothing.

Vesta and Franz rush into the kitchen dragging twin lines of melting snow behind. Franz paws Vivienne then gallops around the kitchen, sliding. Vesta stands behind Velour, reading Clorinda's text.

-Nana, did you do that?

-Do what, honey?

Velour pictures Wilma's broken body on the ground seven or eight stories down, Max's needled, drug-torn form stacked atop it. And her father, too—thin and filled with cancers. Her own dead body, her mother's, her daughter's, the dog's . . .their clothes blowing in the wind and smelling of piss, French perfume, and shit. A saint or an angel arrives—one of these entities her mother apparently believes in—and blesses them, makes the sign of the cross, then continues on. Their bodies, piled high, block traffic. Lou picks the whole mess up in his garbage truck, compacts them until all organs get crushed.

Velour feels herself to be receding, becoming a flattened, paper doll-like version of herself as she zooms out of the room, enervated into two dimensionality. Vesta and Vivienne are the commanding personalities, as she sees it, two feral females with no sense of personal space wearing matching puff sleeves. Velour has heard the accusation before: her mother, Wilma's killer. The words blink into her eyes from the wired walls of the internet, their glassy, effortless momentum. Vesta takes Velour's phone from her. She's holding it like a platter as she reads the tweets aloud from her small palm.

VESTA FURIO

December 12

6:00 a.m.

Vesta Furio is grinding her teeth as she often does in the deep sleep hour before waking. Franz, whom her father named after the artist Franz Kline, sleeps beside her, and the crepuscular sounds emanating from her mouth stir him awake. He leaves the girl be. His dog body, more muscular and furry than her girl body, grasps the morning rhythms. Vesta will wake soon and they'll go downstairs together. Eat, pee, walk, repeat. He quietly licks his ass, then his paws, as Vesta grinds her teeth.

The room is dim. Silent save for the child's bone on bone pulverizing. Franz nudges Vesta and she stirs, stops grinding for a moment, then starts up again. Since forever, the girl has been given to tense nights with sleep broken by bad dreams and bruxism. Recently, she started losing her teeth which are allegedly just temporary *baby* teeth, and she'll be getting adult ones soon enough. *Permanent.* She keeps the small fallen fangs in a silver box with Michael the Archangel on top, a gift from her grandmother, her idol. Those original teeth are the only ones Max Furio knew and so each time a tooth gets uprooted, it feels to Vesta like her father is leaving all over again, her jaw getting as bare and achy as the space around his death.

Max Furio: a tall, capable man with an indistinct face. When Vesta pictures him, she sees a blur where his features should be. He was raised in the city and idealized the country—its vast green peace and long stretches of pretty nothings. Still, he wanted to leave—onward to another world entirely. Vesta has one memory of her father which she counts as all her own—one that she doesn't dare share with her mother or grandmother, for she fears speech will dilute its awesomeness. The memory is part of her central dream machinery, prone to variations which range from terrifying to lovely—

Women in bonnets selling strudel and shoofly pies, old men eating hot dogs with buckets of sauerkraut on top, old men and women whose faces are melting off as they smile at little Vesta—four years old and miniature in dad's arms wearing a black sweater, dad only ever wears black—and today his skin is fast and clear like an angel's—Vesta knows her dad won't ever get old like these sauerkraut people as they walk through a long hallway lined with stalls—dad's clothes change from solid to lava—and Vesta's not wearing any at all—just water—and the hallway is not a hallway but a river flowing into the violent sea—the baubles and antiques the vendors are selling which Vesta finds quite pretty—bubblegum jewelry, glimmering junk, and bright old sweaters that reek of the dead start to float, drown and dad's holding her—but his arms now turn liquid—and over the whole scene—a dog, hanging by its neck—swinging back and forth over the gross, antique-crowded ocean—the dog is Pepper and Pepper looks like a smaller version of Franz—the ceiling is a sky with all the constellations and it's September. Vesta's birthday month. And her lava father points up towards the maiden—that's the one, he says, as the suicided dog swings back and forth above them and dad smiles real big, really big, before telling her all about the vestal virgins—the priestesses of the maiden constellation—they keep the fire of Rome going—are you going to keep the fire going or no? his smile changes to a sinister grin, then he opens his mouth wide—hot, toothless, and pocked with scars

29

When she wakes up, out of breath, her gaze falls on her grandmother's old tarot cards which she had recently taped to the wall opposite her bed. They're arranged in a vertical line:

High Priestess
Strength
Empress
Hermit
Seven of Swords
Hierophant

Vesta finds them beautiful, perfect, much too good to use for fortune telling or for *anything at all*. They are to be kept separate from the dirty world of loose tooths and crooked looks. They are meant to be here—ever beheld by Vesta and Franz, as *art*. Also taped to her wall are several brightly-colored Candyland playing cards. Vesta doesn't care about the game's objective, which has something to do with arriving at a castle of candy. The cards, however—princesses made from pink sugar and mint green princes—she finds stunning. When she tore open the game (a birthday gift from her mother) she immediately decorated her wall with its pieces.

An original Dorothea Tanning painting is also mounted and framed on Vesta's wall: *Tableau Vivant* (1954), a work in which a behemoth fluffy dog, which Vivienne says was the artist's *actual* dog, embraces a naked woman who, depending on Vesta's mood, is peacefully sleeping, excited, terrified, or altogether dead. The dog, too, changes. Sometimes, good and true—a protector. Other times, he means to suck the life out of the woman. The painted dog looks nothing like Franz Kline, though.

Vesta rubs her jaw, then rolls over and embraces Franz, who yawns, dotting her silky purple nightshirt with drool. After their tender morning moments, Franz bounds downstairs, sliding over the old hardwood and annoying Velour. Vesta follows close behind, moving much slower. She makes a point to walk carefully, for a child in her class last year said his grandfather fell down the stairs, cracked his head wide open, and died right there. She has tried and failed to train Franz to go slow. On her way down, Vesta runs her fingers over the intricate wallpaper, its complex designs and eyes and velvety texture, which seems to be living, animated from behind. She whispers into it: *Thirteen days til Christmas*.

∽

The girl pauses at the kitchen's entrance and eyes her mother, sitting in her robe smoking, long hair upclipped in the space Vesta's father died. She wishes to freeze the scene. Vesta is happy they still eat at her father's table. At the flea market that day, Vesta became overwhelmed, suddenly frightened of the old wares shooting musty smells and manned by scary vendors. Trinkets like blackboards and matchboxes, worn and rusted, brummagem and authentic. Her father comforted her. *Magic*, he said. That afternoon, Max Furio put his hand on a white porcelain table bordered with chipped red flowers, closed his eyes, and told his daughter to do the same. They bought the table, along with five white chairs.

She enters the kitchen—*la la la, la la la!*—inside a bubble of joy. She loves the mornings best, especially when she's had a bad dream. Morning washes all the night's silt away and Vesta feels, for a frothy instant, so happy she thinks she'll come apart, limbs pirouetting over the yard. She makes a high pitched screech, only audible to Franz, who jumps. Her joyous surge deflates when she clocks her mother's forlorn face, cheeks sallow as she sucks on a cig.

∽

Girl and dog trot toward town center, twinkling with Christmas lights and a giant plastic candle. The sidewalk into town begins a few feet from the front yard, covered in a light dusting of white snow. *Beautiful*, says

Vesta—then grimaces as she pictures the suicided dog hanging from its neck and swinging above the ocean filled with old junk: disgusting rusted things or pretty portals to other worlds, maybe both. Like the dream dog, Vesta swings. She swings back and forth between elated and sad, at the whimsical mercy of her moods, humming as she makes new lines through immaculate snow, strong Franz yanking her arm. She clicks her tongue against the roof of her mouth to signal *no—come back, be good*, then sing-songs the names of the various downtown establishments as she swings back into something resembling happiness. Town is a rundown four blocks and Vesta loves the look of the shops. Today, their signs tint the snow pink and orange:

> *Christian Book Store*
> *Post Office*
> *Dutch Country Market*
> *Idle Hands Nail Salon*
> *La la la la*
> *Nail Salon*
> *Salon*
> *idle handsnailsalon*
> *salon*
> *idle hands hands hands*
> *nail*
> *sal*
> *on*

On the way back home, Franz marks the snow on repeat, small circles of steaming yellow pee. Standing near the edge of town is Milo in his usual black outfit. With her free hand, Vesta crumples up the fabric of her coat, working it into a ball, nervous.

-Vessssta.

-Hi Milo.

-Nice coat.

-My grandmother made it.

-Vivienne?

-Vivienne Volker, the girl says.

-I just found out your grandpa made those weird dolls.

-Yeah, he was a *famous artist*, Vesta says. She runs her tongue over the vacant spaces in her mouth, then presses her loose tooth back up into its root.

Milo is tall with long stringy hair, and has apparently spent a few years in jail. *Inside*, as she's heard it called. She guesses he's around the same age as Lou, but it's hard to tell, as he seems to Vesta both boyish and old, an alluring quality he shares with the late Max Furio. This morning, his black blazer is wet with snow. They don't talk often, though she seems to run into him constantly. Once, while walking Franz down by the river, which she wasn't *technically* supposed to be doing, Vesta ran into Milo and felt sure he was going to kill her. He didn't do anything at all, didn't even move. No *hello*. Nothing. No. But all that *nothing* and *no* made her feel that *anything* could happen. Milo stirs a silent nebulous sensation that Vesta doesn't have a name for. She dreads running into him while also looking forward to it. A dizzying mix.

-Maybe you'll be a *famous artist*, too, Milo says.

Vesta blinks up at him, smiling and backlit by the daytime neon of Idle Hands Nail Salon. Franz barks at a stray cat, then lunges, nearly pulling her arm out of its socket. Milo grabs the leash and the three of them walk together in silence until the path stops. When Milo gives Franz's leash back to Vesta, their hands touch and Vesta feels a bolt of static electricity. She watches him head back into town, weight forward and hands in pockets, walking with a slight bounce.

Maybe you'll be a famous artist, too, Vesta repeats as she mimics his walk, bouncing alongside Franz all the way back to the house. When she enters the kitchen, her mother is slumped over her phone looking disturbed and Vesta's Milo halo fades, quickly replaced by her paralytic fear of bad news.

The girl swivels around, turning to face the living room, wallpaper eyeballs watching her every move.

She reads the words on her mother's phone, body tingling as her face flushes.

Vesta looks at her grandmother, whose strange and comforting smells ribbon around, permeate the world—French perfume, smoke, and something new.

VIVIENNE VOLKER

December 12

6:00 a.m.

Sleeping with the window open and dreaming of rhythmic crickets inside a whirl of broken garments, garments made of scraps and shaped into bustiers, crinolines, trousers, gloves, jackets. Clothes for the misshapen and deformed. Wool and silk coverings for nubs, a set of trousers with four leg holes, and a bra with one cup, a skinny boa made from pubic hair. Vivienne herself is in the center of the tornado, unspooling. Almost gone.

Hans Bellmer and Wilma Lang, both of whom she's been dreaming of since July, are also caught in the whirl. Plus Vesta and Velour—their hair whipped by wind. They look like her daughter and granddaughter, but speak French and stare at Viv as though she's a stranger. *Qui es-tu? Qu'est ce que tu regardes?* Vivienne's signature winter coat ties her to earth, preventing her from getting swept away. Underneath the jacket's dream-train, longer and more billowy than her actual jacket are the dolls those garments are meant for. They want to be taken care of. Everything spins.

~

Vivienne is a good sleeper. On her side. Face placid. Dreams, even when terrible, rarely wake her. At eighty-two, she appears healthful and unencumbered, people frequently mistaking her for a woman much younger. Vivienne attributes her youthful looks to quitting art and its worlds back in the 1970s. Since that time, things have reversed. She was old back then —those days in Paris. In her post-art life, she's worked in Europe and America as a seamstress, altering and mending the stuff of others. Though her face's age is hard to read, her hands tell all: liver spotted, veiny, arthritic, uncanny, like she's wearing gloves made from the skin of an elderly woman, someone she hasn't yet met.

Back when she was writing books and sewing fabric sculptures to be displayed and considered by a public, she felt *inhabited* by a force which sucked out portions of her and replaced them, bit by bit, with more amplified, inflated energies. When Lou or Velour show her old pictures of herself on the internet (how did they get there?) she sees a woman overfull: wildeyed and forlorn, bolded and underscored. Ever since she stopped—just, *stopped*—she's been working on evacuating herself, whittling herself down, humbler and more simple. Even so, she's excited for the group show.

Just before she wakes, there's a dog with wings, a galloping pony, and that familiarly exhilarating *inhabited* feeling. When her eyes open, they land on the sky just beyond the window. The sun's only just beginning to rise, which means she woke up too early. *Not a good sign.* She's thinking again about the scraps of Parisian trash she fashioned those doll clothes from so many decades ago.

She looks at Lou's side of the bed, empty. He left for work two hours ago. She suspects their shared affinity for trash is what drew them together. Not every sanitation worker is as passionate or knowledgeable about scraps as Lou. She runs her palm over his imprint on the peach-colored sheet, then blinks into the backyard's green. She smells Lou's side of the bed—young, alive. Though she considers herself to have impeccable hygiene, much better than her daughter's, Vivienne knows she reeks of death—diseased grass, old urine, decrepit feathers.

She sits up in bed, flicks on the green glass lamp, lights a clove cigarette, and sprays Miss Dior perfume on her wrists. She has to pee. Vivienne's begun, these past few months, to think of every pee as her final one. For now, she'll hold it. Even though Velour insists on keeping haunted art from Viv's past all around the house—a drawing by Hans in the kitchen, a collage by Vivienne in the living room, the doll in the basement—she likes living here, and thinks of it as a kind of reward for any good she's done in her life, which she senses might be over soon.

The upcoming show at the NAT, she regards as a kind of last hoorah, and also as a spiritual test she's already failed. She's allowed herself to be affected by recognition: infiltrated and distended. *FORGOTTEN WOMEN SURREALISTS*? Who, exactly, had forgotten her and all those dead women? And who was supposed to remember now? Why? She looks at the Virgin Mary figurine next to her bed, closes her eyes, takes a drag of her cigarette, and prays.

Hail Mary
Full of Grace
The Lord is with thee.
Blessed art thou among women,
and blessed is the fruit
of thy womb, Jesus.
Holy Mary,
Mother of God,
pray for us sinners now,
and at the hour of our death.
Amen.

She says the prayer two more times, then recalls the first time she saw Lou hanging from the back of a garbage truck in town. Despite his line of work, he smells like the fuzz on a newborn baby's head. She respects people who do one thing very well. Hans and his dolls. Lou and his knowledge of how to dispose of things. Velour and her apocalyptic preoccupation with endings. Vesta and her melancholic eye, her desire to freeze-frame the world's constant moves. And her own self—whoever that was—an old woman-child with a penchant for making garments out of anything.

Hubris blocks grace, as Vivienne well knows, but since the NAT called a few months ago asking if she'd be part of their big show, Vivienne has felt special again—the twirling world coated in creation's cool residue, images upon images upon images ad nauseum. She stubs out her cigarette and forces herself out of bed, walks over to her vanity and looks in the mirror, opening and closing her mouth and shaking her head. Teeth stained, skin filled with lines. She throws her hair up into a bun and dabs more perfume behind her ears—a cheaper American one called Design—to mask any rot. She walks to the toilet and pees, feeling the warm liquid leave her body and looking down at the stream, meditating on its color, yellow as her perfume. Sighs.

∼

Weeks ago, Vesta made Vivienne promise to take the stairs carefully, slower than she thinks humanly possible. Vivienne complies, larghetto down the narrow spiral staircase. As she makes her funereal descent into the land below, her legs grow heavy and she reflects on her daughter's home, its gothic, maximalist décor an extra-ness which Vivienne reads as a reaction against growing up inside her own aesthetic anorexia. The house is like a magnetic basin—holding onto entities as they hang indefinitely in its orbital rotation. Lou, for instance. Max. Viv. And Velour, the house mistress, whom Vivienne believes is just a few *I'd rather not go out todays* away from being a shut-in.

Her daughter, per usual, is at the shiny white kitchen table in her dead husband's chair, smoking his brand. Velour is earth. Little Vesta,

38

on the other hand, is air. Her granddaughter has a way of seeming to be *everywhere*—vapor of Vesta fills the house and makes bearable the charged space between Vivienne and her daughter. Vesta is like Hermes, a quick and curious messenger sent to commune between them, between the house and the world, between this world and the other ones.

Velour in her eponymous robe, a white garment growing ferns and spores and dirt, trailing behind her and billowing toward the field and ' the woods beyond and beyond and beyond. Velour growing old. Velour with the little girl at her feet, and the little girl's dog. Old, stained, storied hardwood underneath. The dog has wings and mad eyes. Talons that grip the wood, and the wood floors, like the dog and the girl and the mother are one with the eye-covered interior.

Vesta speaks. Says her dream. A dog killing herself. Another corridor. *What's wrong with showing a kid a Bergman movie. All children are traumatized from the jump.* It's called *being born*. Velour, hair tangled with sticks, mud, and old scraps of fabric, joins with the landscape. Vivienne shakes her head while dragging on her clove, then exhales the smoke while reciting in her head another Hail Mary to make the bad thoughts go.

The entire downstairs, its living and waking world, all wrapped up in the natural disaster of a dream. Her arms are buzzing with numbness as the other zone breaks into this one, smashed glass. Demolition and divagation. There's nothing she can do. That much, Vivienne knows, sees. *Eine Kleine Nachtmusik* overtakes Vivienne's Hail Mary, a song on sinister slow repeat.

No matter, no matter, Vivienne thinks.
A little night music, a little night music, a little night music, music in the night—

—what was the dog in the dream hanging from? Why dig for dirty details,
Velour sneers, blowing smoke in Viv's eye. Why not, Vivienne shoots back. The dog
was hanging from a beautiful silk ribbon. That part makes Vivienne shiver. She looks

out into the creeping field—the land surrounding this house is fine—especially when coated in thin pure clean snow as now—still falling—but not as beautiful as Velour thinks—

—at church, Viv will go to confession. Will pray for the ribbons of music to go away. Maybe the girls will come with her today. Don't forget rosary beads. Vesta and Franz have gone and come back, happy for the moment. Just let the kid get her nails done—she's not too young.

Vesta, in her trembly voice, reads a note written about Vivienne on the internet—

Velour says the note has gone viral—

Did you kill someone?—all those years ago?

The little girl wants to know.

THE RIBBON IS A ROAD: THE LIFE & WORK OF VIVIENNE VOLKER

CONTENT WARNING

The following video contains material that may be harmful or traumatizing to some audiences.

www.youtube.com
Uploaded:
December 16 at 9:44 p.m.
Eda Singer
29 minutes

[A compilation of images: paintings, drawings, sculptures, and clips of writing by Vivienne Volker play over slow electronic music. Photographs from the artist's life, including pictures of Volker, her daughter Velour Bellmer, her lover Hans Bellmer, and Hans's wife Wilma Lang, are interspersed with images of the work.]

<VIDEO DESCRIPTION>

I've compiled this montage as a tribute to the art and life of Vivienne Volker in the wake of the NAT Museum removing her work from the upcoming exhibition. I'm a longtime fan and student of Volker's work and have studied her life extensively, along with the works and lives of Hans Bellmer and Wilma Lang, whom hers was so entangled with. As far as I know, this is the first video compilation of its kind. For those of you unfamiliar with the recent controversy, I'm including the NAT's statement below, followed by my attempt at a brief biography of Volker and a description of my own relationship to her art.

45

"Due to concerns about the potentially harmful nature of Volker's work, along with serious allegations involving the artist's past, namely her involvement in the suicide of Wilma Lang, a fellow artist whose work is also included in our upcoming show, we are redacting Vivienne Volker's work from *Forgotten Women Surrealists*. However, this is not an act of censorship. At the NAT Museum, we seek to foster artistic freedom in an atmosphere of safety. Wherever possible, we seek to reduce art-induced distress. When we reached out to Ms. Volker for answers, we received no clarification. Due to the severity of the allegations surrounding Volker's personal history alongside the number of disturbances expressed around the violent nature of her work, we have made the difficult decision to remove Volker's *Dressing the Dolls* sculptures from the show. *Forgotten Women Surrealists* will be on view from March 22nd through June 24th. Best wishes for a happy new year. We hope to see you at the museum."

VIVIENNE VOLKER was a hard-to-categorize visual artist and writer often associated with Surrealism. Fabric and language, textile and text, were her main materials. Her books include an epistolary novel entitled *Seeing Hands* (1965), the collection of poetry *Objects of Love* (1970), and a delirious book of prose, *The Machine-Gunneress in a State of Grace* (1977). Volker's work shapeshifts as it sifts through the language and art of others in order to channel and unlock new worlds, resulting in uncanny sculptures made from what's been discarded.

Born in Philadelphia, Pennsylvania in 1940, Volker crisscrossed America and Europe for much of her life, living in New York City, Los Angeles, France, and Germany while working as a seamstress before moving to a small town in Pennsylvania a few years ago. Her most productive and prominent decade was the 1970s, especially 1970-1975, while living with Hans Bellmer.

During this time, she made a series of twenty-seven sculptures entitled *Dressing the Dolls*, hand sewn garments inspired by the mutilated shapes of Bellmer's infamous doll sculptures. One can view them as extensions of the dolls or as discreet entities unto themselves. Volker disappeared from artistic circles and the public eye shortly after *The Machine-Gunneress in a State of Grace* (1977) was published, a book which documents both her relationship with Bellmer during the years leading up to his death in 1975 and the trials of raising their daughter, Velour, born a few months after Bellmer's passing.

I first read *The Machine-Gunneress in a State of Grace* (1977) as a teen. A series of neuralgic and ecstatic entries on her love affair with Bellmer, the book disturbed and comforted me. Named for a sculpture by Hans Bellmer in which a life-sized doll-like is fractured and held together with mechanical joints, the book itself is as discombobulated and anarchic as the sculpture. Her final book was, among other things, a hymn to *him* and the various states of grace she found while in mourning, communing with his ghost. Death is never the end, the book says.

Although received with excitement upon its initial publication by a small circle of artists, *The Machine-Gunneress in a State of Grace* and Volker's other books have long been out of print. Her paintings and sculptures are difficult to find and her name, until this scandal, abandoned. The NAT Museum has cast her work out of the show due to its "needlessly violent nature" and a rumor. I hope this video will be a landing pad for those interested in Vivienne Volker, the artist and the woman. **[collapse]**

Vivienne

I was in my thirties. We loved that painting by Delacroix, the one of a tiger attacking a wild horse. I printed the scene on fabric and made a dress. I wore it to this party in Paris. It must have been late summer when I met him and it felt like that painting. Who was the tiger and who the horse? He told me he couldn't tell if I liked him, and that excited him to no end. I sewed until my hands hurt and I hated the sun, which seemed to taunt me—urging me outside to match its fabulosity. It lit my own good and evil—revealing shade, shadow.

Video

@dressedinf1nitud3
Stunning and mesmerizing
I felt like I was taken to a new planet

@lozenge2
FINALLY

@bruun3
glorified rags

@breadnbutts
volker, ahead of her time
hans looks like undertaker
wilma jumped from what window
@ 10:33: skirt made from parachute?

@lit7703
WHO?

@redstill
The artist Wilma Lang was Hans Bellmer's lover, maybe wife?
She was psychwarded throughout her life.
Then jumped from his window.
The maker of this video conveniently
left that part out of her slanted bio.
Then, Vivienne moved in, lived w Hans
until his death in 1975.
Shortly after he croaked, their daughter Velour was born . . .
[more]

@bruun3
wld let him take me under

@7855309*
who made the tiger dress
she's wearing at 12:22 min?

@JesusisLord8181
PASS THRU EVIL
TO ARRIVE
PARADISE !

@lit7703
Hans was 40 years VV's senior

@lit7703
*38 yrs

@reactoronica
if you support Vivienne
blood on your hands

@heyfivebux
shes dead

@systemprocessings
WRONG, she is ALIVE

@user6652001
absurd logic

@89vvvc
wrong to stay silent
about the violence
of V*v*enne V*lker
her "life and work"
ha ha what a joke

@dressedinf1nitud3
austere euphoria
already gone
rejoining the kingdom

@lit7703
is she guilty or

Vivienne

A body walking a long satin ribbon toward oblivion, night music. We'd speak about the act lightly, laughing hysterically. Naturally, nothing was funnier than offing oneself or another, as nothing more terrible. Now, infinities of windows. To where, I don't know. By the time I moved in with him, Hans was largely bedridden. I called him a dirty saint, a sick mystic. After his death, if I wasn't so pregnant, I might have jumped into the grave with him. Years prior to any of this, I wore that Delacroix painting around me, printed onto my scrap dress, at a party on ludes as I danced in slow motion to The Doors. So young I felt OLD. The outfit prohibited movement. My body was thin and stiff, a bridge, the horizontal line between the year he was born and the year he died.

Video

@fashionvictem (edited)
shocked , amazed , wonder , be mesmerized ,,, all in one !!!!!

@anonagain
for those who didn't exist
that era had less
mannerless automatons
truly the good

@ggn5maryann
ruched dress and mud bra
9:00: Georges Bataille?

@frockconsciousva
she presaged 90s
minimalism
outside all day
comfy and effortless
we want nothing
to do with your ways
leave us alone
clean fucking slate

@reactoronica
she's alive in decrepit Pennsylvania
unsure how to reach us mayb

@lemoncellobabey
@ 8 like min into the vid
most graceful sculpture
Rest In Peace Beauty

@fortysomething
vivienne is not dead
Oh that I had
wings of a dove

@writehandwoman
DO BETTER!
she. Is. A.
PREDATOR
bird of prey
GET IT? alarming
howwever i find it borderline tragic
we cant see how her art
would have evolved
would be

@lemoncellobabey
who got all her stuff

@lavano
14 min
her clothing turns dolls into
harpies
more/less human
birds with the heads
of maidens

@ubernono
THEY ARE ALL DEAD
BURIED WHERE?

@stalled6
I've told this story elsewhere but, the first time I saw her
was at Gare de Lyon.
On that morning in the late 70s, she was waiting for a train
with her little girl.
She stood close to me on the track
as we waited for the same train to take us away.

@lalabrandlando
exploitative
metal rod meant to go
through the neck (?!) impalement etc
hair feathers plastic tangled
women as roadkill
women on the ground
given bird beaks
swooping downnnnnnnnn
sux

@obitchuary
tho that gravitydefyingdress
"to destroy the past is the only criminal act :)" who said dat?
cages, restraints
this clothing is meant to make the dolls
even more misshapen deranged etc correct?

@vbl5f
those who murder themselves are punished
in the 7th ring of hell
consigned to be tortured in woods
wood of suicides
insatiable creepy
hehe

@emmawuttt
while at times oddly lovely,
this video says nothing
THE WIND
KEEPS SCREAMING

Vivienne

In the silver river, I'm a pony. Clothesless and roaming. Precisely when you run your fingers over the stitches. Bound bone and tremendous ditches are shocked as they clock your helmet and black trench coat. You were a loaded Giotto. Then in the shallow yellow part, you needle wet threads into my fell coat. When I come to, we're in the portion of a home which receives more light, near a window from which no one has jumped. Equal parts monastery and industry. In the parlor at last, we can speak. I was cast off the street. I was told to walk in circles to the calliope derangement of circus music. In a far-off arrondissement, I was dead. The sky showed a montage—every outfit I wore, every time I swooped, vulture-like. From remnants, I sewed a cream-colored gown of feathers, skin, and hair that covered everyone—city, river, town. Then galloped past pink and orange clothes bodiless on racks. Hay and dirt on the highway. Pepto-Bismol coated shoes. Recherché and unseemly flashes made white the hay. I believe I was living. Lit cymbals and plastic crowns. Fur against faux fur. Inside a viscose night which clung to the coming day, when we'd go to a party. With one shaking hand, you managed to steady me. Beyond humanly. With the other, you held then released a pink balloon. Years later, it landed dirty and sweet on a street in Pennsylvania. Hail Mary, full of grace.

Video

@simontides
yawn

@matthew89036
I WAS ALLOWED TO SEE AN ANGEL.
4 wheels, 10 wings, and hundreds of eyes

@aposteriori74
As an artist working in the Surrealist mode, I am certain
Vivienne is aware of Breton's famous formulation, and her
work does seem to strive for the 'systematic derangement
of all the senses.' However, we should investigate the
places where Vivienne's (and our own) biases reside within
and around these sensorial mix-ups. While I am grateful
for this video compilation, I am also heartened by the
NAT's decision to omit Vivienne's work and replace it with
nothing at all, asking us to stare into the silence of the
gap and find a new way forward. I hope Vivienne (and you
all here) will consider doing the same. I have a number of
texts I'd love to recommend to her. Does anyone happen
to have her email address?

@alanlapoupee
pissing into the abyss? yawl need to look at yr lives

@vbl5f
harpies not angels
insatiable
the very existence of Vivienne is offensive, fucked

[this comment has been removed]

@sarahbarnes
compelling essay in artnews today arguing against
platforming vv's work out of respect and reverence for
those she hurt, and those she may hurt in the future

Vivienne

*I began sewing. Something worked in me, without me. He'd watch
my hands sew. He said hands could see better than eyes and that
I should spend all my days in a state of seeing-sewing. I agreed. In
and out—in and out—coalescing and diverging bodies and roads.*

Video

@simontides
she should get g*ng r*ped

@momminearest004
Vivienne goes to my church.
I see her each week.
She is odd but
does not deserve
the above. Does anyone?

[this comment has been removed]

@dressedinf1nitud3
TWO WINGS COVER ME, WITH TWO WINGS I SEE.
Can I communicate with you via letter? Our secrets are
indecipherable, but I want a record nonetheless. Can we
do it without the platforms? I was needing to address you
ASAP but as yet couldn't this wasn't invented you're so good
I want you to have everything you want in life man oh man
you have my attention and my respect I'm not religious in
any way but I am broken and messages can move between
two entities perched atop some commonality let's not let it
ruin us—all these ways to make someone look bad and evil
before knowing them. The fallen angels sing common sense
confuses the hell out of some people I look for you save
western civilization? There was violence—horrifying—and I
survived—my advice? Canoe. Or, just . . .do something! Pull
self out of self, like Keep Moving. Give yourself a view, go
outside. Exit comments but who am I to tlk. Disrespecting
trends and Beliefs can be healthy. Society, is this it? if you

are sad, for instance, backpack. sail, join a club, whatever, be relentless—all best wishes. I wanted to be an assistant—your cosmic custodian, blessed. What is the difference between an assistant and an angel and a bird with a girl's head? Imagine how weak and Infantile you have to be in order to b traumatized after looking at this shit! See how wwhat's acceptable has been limited? Se how within that spectrem you think freedom!...? You fools aren't going to last 1 day after all this shit collapses. Tyranny!!! The angels turn to harpies. Cast out or chosen to flow from clarity to static, vulturous. Some wings are covered in real eyes. Whatever. How can I help you? I mean, really, how can i? **[collapse]**

@MN9900
Incidentally, I once was in her residence. It resembled a crowded tomb—claustrophobic. I was a teen, gaga over all those weirdos. And Vivienne took me under her wing. The space was strewn with fabric scraps, drawings of insane angels, the biblical kind with thousands of eyes, wheels. Hard to imagine living there at all.

@nicorettela
Hi! Michel? Is that you? It's Nicolette.
I was around the scene then.
I heard Viv's work had been annihilated.
Haven't seen it or her in ages. I ended up here.

@MN9900
Nicolette! Mais bien sur!
Is there a way to send a message directly?
I don't want to share my contact info with this whole group, no offense.

@gbno8xz
I AM OFFENDED

@nicorettela
Hi Michel @MN9900—yes,
I messaged you. I hope you got it . . . .

@lamentations77041
Angel Gabriel came to me on a treadmill at the gym.
He was lit-up, divine, terrifying. I stopped suddenly and
that emergency belt halted me, whiplashed me onto the
ground. These artworks speak to my experience directly.
Thank you, Miss Volker, whoever you are!! Bless.

@survbapmessage
i performed open heart surgery but i am not a surgeon
never went to med school but i knew i could
do it the patient was Hans Bellmer
my hands had eyes and they were unsanitized
Volker stood over me watching my work
unimpressed hopeful Wilma was there, too
all died brutally me included

@fastmannequin
ever had sexxx with a surrealist?

[this comment has been removed]

@jordanlo
FASCIST

63

@elliemental
theres 1 recent photo of her in colorado
or wherever she lives shes wearing v cool black coat
looks frailer than joan didion

@marindab
fascist or not, the woman was an icon saw her once in France
and she was wearing an old pair of stockings as a shirt it looked
tremendous i tried to copy the look an failedn

@alejandravee8
hi after seeing the slide where V. Volker writes about her
relationship with H. Bellmer as an almost post-verbal
frequency (?) moving between bodies and changing their
veryy forms i'm now convinced i ve never been in an
actual relationship

@seventyseventy
how r u going to counter totalitarianism
with dolls and clothes?
this woman is not alive
SPLAT she died
send them ALL to an island !!!1

[this comment has been removed]

@bracelet1984
i love the image where Hans and Viv are looking
into the distance
i think they're looking out that window

@seventyseventy
wanted to go outside

@alejandravee8
no @seventyseventy you are thinking of Wilma Lang and
this vid is about Vivienne Volker (the lover he had AFTER!!)
the final girl, so to speak Vivienne did not jump out of a
window tho she may have pushed(?) Wilma or maybe
even pushed others, idk, like somehow talked people
into jumping, so says the internet is there a statute of
limitations shite like this

@holyroamerz
dis video makes me wanna jump out window
who else did she kill?

@baroqueha
yall have a lack of basic reading comprehension lol

@seventyseventy
deleuze jumped from his window in Paris too
this pressure is UN IV ER SAL!
even the gorgeous model Gisele
has said she fantasized
about doing the same
and dont forget the poet Laura Riding
(lover of ROBERT GRAVES)
fell or was pushed (big maybe)
i was roamin around
led here by the algorithm

@poemextra
THREADED INTO THE CAPE WAS AN EYE
AND A TONGUE FOR EVERY HUMAN

@bossnjy
Paranoiac

[this comment has been removed]

@unmemory2
I'm here to support the forgotten and those who've exterminated themselves or who've been exterminated by others. I've been a fan of Vivienne's for years, and I own all three of her books. In my experience, the work is quite healing. During my forced hospitalization, it was medicine . . . .
[more]

@labn4eeeeeeeeeeeeek
fuckng larpy

Stunning and mesmerizing
I felt like I was taken to a new planet

LARS

December 16
New York, New York
9:44 p.m.

Eyes burning from the blue light of his screen, Lars Arden has been in scheming mode for hours. On his desk: scribbled notes and three chewed-up bodega coffee cups. One spilt on a novel he's been intermittently reading, a story about gentrification in New York City that an acquaintance had recommended. Lars tosses the soaked book onto the gallery floor and it makes a spongy thud. He runs his hand up his arm, tightening his muscles and feeling the veins. He's recently upped his workout regimen, taking five spin classes per week, plus heavier weights. He twists around in his swivel chair, regarding the wet novel before looking out the large glass gallery window at the yellow, red, and white haze of downtown.

Ding—

He swivels back around to face the screen. A new video about Vivienne Volker was just uploaded by some girl. *Good sign, good—yes. Fuck! Fifty views in minute one? And climbing—okay—cool*—he turns around again, dizzily flashing to a dream scenario wherein "Lars Arden's Gallery X goes viral for showing Vivienne Volker's brilliant and controversial work, NAT Museum expresses regret, embarrassment!" He's soaring high high high on the demented sewn wings of Vivienne Volker, a name he heard for the first time only recently.

It's nearly 10 p.m., which means Lars has been tracking the Vivienne drama for twelve hours. He wheels around, the barren eggshell gallery walls blurring. He moves faster, pushing his feet off the shiny floor as he waits to hear back from Clorinda.

He picks up his phone and reviews their text conversation from earlier:

CLORINDA 11:50am
You should take this on:

"Due to concerns about the potentially harmful nature of Volker's work, along with serious allegations involving Volker's past, namely her involvement in the suicide of Wilma Lang, a fellow artist whose work is also included in our upcoming show, we are redacting Volker's work from Forgotten Women Surrealists."

LARS 11:50am
totally
agree
been following the story

CLORINDA 11:51am
youll get eyes

LARS 11:51am
what do you think
of her work

CLORINDA 11:51am
some claim the doll clothes are more fuckedup
than Bellmer's dolls
cld play that up

LARS 11:51am
true true

CLORINDA 11:52am
vivienne's daughter is an old friend
maybe we can be the first to scoop her up
look at Vivienne's work and confirm that
youll be willing to stand by it

LARS 11:52am
God you know everyone!
how i love you
doing further research
ALL DAY

CLORINDA 11:52 am
just texted Velour
her daughter

LARS 11:52am
what's her deal

CLORINDA 11:53am
vivienne or velour?

LARS 11:54 am
either both

CLORINDA 11:54am

dropouts

living in Pennsylvania

velour is like world's foremost scholar on her parents werk

but won't publish

recluse

LARS 11:54am

do they have any Bellmers

CLORINDA 11:54am

V never speaks of it

idk

LARS 11:54am

just googled her

CLORINDA 11:54am

former party girl

LARS 11:55am

i see!

looking at a pic of her and jfk jr . . .

CLORINDA 11:56am

she used to know everyone

now shes fucked

LARS 11:57am

i bet u bonded over the fact that you both

have parents with window drama

CLORINDA 11:58am
her husband OD'd

LARS 11:59am
when?

CLORINDA 12:00pm
few years ago
they disappeared
nowhere
velour was like me
NEVER wanted kids
near the bitter end popped one out

LARS 12:00pm
single mom

CLORINDA 12:01pm
Velour is typing . . . .

LARS 12:12pm
anything yet?!!!
THE SUSPENSE

CLORINDA 12:14pm
no
these women are skittish
best not to PUSH
will let you kno when she texts

~

Lars Arden met Clorinda Salazar, a socialite moonlighting as a stylist and internet writer, at a coffee shop a few years ago when they struck up a conversation about an article she was writing entitled "Sexualities You Didn't Know Existed." Clorinda's reputation preceded her, and Lars felt she lived up to the hype: a gorgeous, big chested redhead with an encyclopedic knowledge of who and what was *in*. The daughter of the late abstract expressionist known simply as Salazar, a painter who won notoriety amongst the downtown set and beyond when he allegedly pushed his wife, the artist Paulina Paz, from her studio window onto the sidewalk. After she woke from a brief coma following the six-story fall, she didn't press charges and their careers flourished.

Their only child, Clorinda, was about ten years older than Lars, but looked much younger. When she came up to him unexpectedly, asking if he identified as *any weird sexuality*, he was so taken by her that he'd blurted out, *um, demisexual*, although he had no idea what it meant. Clo smiled: *I don't have one of those yet!* After she agreed to interview him the next day, he pulled up the definition on his phone: *Demisexuals are only aroused by those with whom they have a strong emotional bond.*

Lars takes a final swig of his cold black coffee, cracks his neck, and reads Eda Singer's biography of Vivienne beneath the YouTube video that he hopes will serve as a solid intro to the old woman's art. He hesitates to press PLAY, for fear he'll hate Vivienne's work, which he's already fantasizing about selling. Lars's latest goal: to *believe in* and *be moved by* the work Gallery X shows. But he's picky, and the gallery walls have been bare for three months. His cursor hovers over the play button and his mind races. If Vivienne agrees to show those old doll clothes in this space, he'll need to act fast—ride the wave of Viv's virality. There'll be a new cursed cultural object in the art news soon and no one will give a shit about her berserk garments and alleged criminality.

He'll have his crew do a speedy install and make a plan—something electric and scandalous to jolt the space awake after its recent sleepiness. Lars's heart pounds the way it pounds when he knows he's circling something major and bright. Perhaps Gallery X can show some lost works of Hans Bellmer. Shit, maybe Velour has some art of her own. Lars could become the glowing representative of the Bellmer-Volker clan, delivering their hidden genius to the world, piece by piece, show by show, forevermore. He'd be committing an act of great service, no?

He turns away from the screen, spinning around and around in his chair. Yes, an act of great service: rehoming the grotesque aesthetics of Volker, a forgotten artist burned at the internet's stake, which might help Gallery X—and Lars—grow *souls*. Ever since he'd read Marguerite Porete's mystical book for which she got burned at the literal stake in fourteenth century Paris, *The Mirror of Simple Souls*, he hasn't been able to shake the notion of *growing a soul—a simple soul*. He was immediately drawn to the book, its obscure, medieval instructions and stern words about annihilation of the self and direct union with the divine. Lars relates. He annihilates himself every day.

Lars's fourth wind is peaking. He stands up and does a little dance: punching the air, moving his shoulders up and down. Then he sits back down and rolls toward the screen. Checks his phone. No word from Clo. He gets up again: stretches, does twenty low lunges, then sits back down, opening a new tab.

VELOUR BELLMER. He says the name aloud as he types her into the search bar and clicks through a slew of images from the '90s and early aughts. He's pregaming for the main event—the video compilation of Vivienne's work. To delay what he's looking forward to is good. In the images, Velour has tangled blondish hair and often wears quirky, costumed outfits: sequined dress, goth shrug, huge platform boots with lace stockings and a leotard. Her garish clothes offset by the fact that she's never smiling. Sad and hot, thinks Lars, clicking.

In one image, she's with Clorinda. In another, a strung-out looking blonde dude. In another, a slew of models. In another, a crowd of glamorous people in minidresses and boxy suits Lars half-recognizes. Though her name is listed in the image descriptions, she's an afterthought, nearly gone, a forlorn clown whose semi-recognizable last name reverberates behind far famouser entities. There are no recent images, nothing at all from the past decade. Lars contemplates jacking off to the image of Velour and Clorinda on a couch in a club that was long ago shut down. He unzips his black Rick Owens pants and touches his cock, its teardrop of precum. *No, stay focused.* He zips back up.

Still delaying the video, Lars sits up tall and clicks through pictures of Hans Bellmer's sculptures. A giant doll, machinic and bizarre, assembled and disassembled, deranging its woman-girl shape. The artist, according to this website, thought of the doll as a *sentence*—a sentence to be formed and deformed, broken up into other language. To Lars, the dolls are uglier *and* more beautiful than anything Salazar's ever done. He's always been a fan of Bellmer, particularly of the second doll he made—shown here in various dismembered and tweaky positions, a response to the horrors of the Nazi regime.

What is the difference between an artist and a killer? Lars wonders aloud as he swivels. Must be something about the *soul*? Fabric and plastic, flesh and bone. He clicks through more images, eyes watering, dizzy. His knowledge of art is ad hoc and he fancies himself a renegade and an outsider. Clorinda is one of his beautiful bridges *in*. And soon: Vivienne.

∾

Now, Lars clicks between eight open internet windows. Every few minutes, he gazes out the gallery window into the city's bright blackness. The street is empty save for one homeless guy, a dark mound with a red umbrella and junk-filled rucksack, moving its hand in a slo-mo circle, miming the application of lipstick.

Finally, he presses PLAY on Eda Singer's video compilation of Vivienne's work and turns the volume all the way up, with music as creepy as the homeless guy outside, a slow dubstep with soft and child-like voices which sound like they're trapped in little vials clanking quietly against one another. (Distant shrieks and birds struggling to flutter their wings.) In the first image, Vivienne's young and smiling. Lars leans back, hands behind head.

Now, a sculpture: maroon fabric, wooly and velvet, with four legs and billowing iridescent material overflowing the pockets, cascading wavelike onto the floor. It reminds Lars of intestines, like the doll's insides are on the outside and the image clouds over, whitening. Drum machine. Some beats on repeat. Lars closes his eyes. The guts disappear into the sea. He opens his eyes to an image of Vivienne and Velour, both dressed in black and standing beside a hideous painting. On the bottom of the image in blue pen: *1977, Paris.* Vivienne is holding Velour while looking over her shoulder into a blotch of red.

Mother and daughter fade into a drawing wherein a miniature girl— too small to be living, too real to be a doll—lies under a sewing machine's silver needle, almost lanced. Lars leans in. The girl, a piece of fabric getting stitched. He can feel his dick getting softer and softer, retracting into his body, a zoom lens pulling back. Now, Lars is Hans. Vivienne opens the door and smiles at him, her face beaming and blameless as a little kid's. She reaches into his olden and bloated innards. *What've you been working on? Nothing. May I use you as material? May I use your material? Do you think you are capable of performing—you know—sexually—though you're so old and sickly? Yes, I have one more in me. Okay, let's make something. A baby?*

His eyes flutter open, mouth slack and drooling. Half-hard now. Vivienne is smoking a long black clove under a tall palm, face painted with gray eyeshadow and red lipstick, eyes wide and ponderous. The next picture features one of Volker's doll sculptures. As it materializes, the doll blots out Vivienne's red pout and startles Lars. He's himself again— no longer Hans. An outfit made of plastic with one thin ribbon of pink fabric, felt or wool, running down the center like a gutter, meant to line the doll's spine, he guesses. Do dolls have spines? A maroon codpiece dangles off the front, a crude rendering of a cock and balls. Lars chuckles.

Another image. Vivienne younger, hunched over, sewing. She's wearing black in a long dark room, her pink lipstick a shock in the obsidian hall. Hanging on the walls all around her small body are drawings. Lars leans forward, wipes his mouth, pauses the video, and zooms in. The drawings look like barbaric surveillance filled with lidless eyeballs scribbled onto amorphous figures with wings and hair. He enlarges Vivienne's image, her long face weathered, her hands remarkably small, wielding a silver needle like a delicate feminine weapon.

He drifts off as the images flicker and glitter across his face and clothing. A long purple coat cinched by two silky brown bras, each with only one breast cup. One is up top near the neck and the other hangs down near the feet, meant for a doll with rogue boobs. Lars shakes his head. This bitch was *on one*, he says. The bra straps bunch the fabric into waveforms. *Beautiful*, he says. He burps. Vivienne and baby Velour stand in a wide field: white, blue, purple water roaring toward them. Red birds overhead.

Lars is in the arms of his own mother in an arena of sinister and impossible wallpaper and sky, florals and eyes. She's rocking him back and forth in constant motion before an ocean painted by Vivienne, both of them dressed in her twisted garments. His mother in a bright blue jumpsuit with white stitches and floppy bird wings and little Lars in a red onesie with a velvet dick-shaped pocket sewn onto the stomach, flaccid and waving in the wind. Mother and child are connected by a large metal sewing needle running from one jumpsuit to the other, shoved through their tummies.

Images of Vivienne, Velour, and doll clothes play at a quicker clip as Lars blinks, rubbing his eyes with trembling hands. The comments are buzzing, an energized mix of vitriol, praise, and nonsense. The demented chorus makes Lars giddy. He howls.

brilliant!
taken to another world
creepy, terrible, justice for Vivienne

is this woman alive or dead
transphobe, bigot
murderer
radical, transcendent
WHO DIS?
why the little cock-shaped pockets?!
hahaha hilarious
such negative capability
mother-child impalement
yikes
DOES ANYBODY REMEMBER LAUGHTER
better left to the dustbin
would fuck her
RIP!
She's not dead
living in the sticks

Lars plays the video again from the beginning. Exhausted, he thinks of his mother, gone. And his father, uptown. And his dad's cash (largely gone) which had backed Gallery X. The ocean is gone. The garments are gone. The giant sewing needle and pubic hair and bird wings and wallpaper, gone gone gone. Just the white cube of an empty art room and Lars in the middle, dressed in all black: shirt, jacket, and combat boots.

In the beginning, Clorinda was impressed because Lars was one of the few guys she didn't have to dress. And she didn't even get upset when he revealed he was not a demisexual. In fact, she was relieved: *what kind of psycho needs to have an emotional connection with someone in order to feel physical attraction?* She didn't need him for the piece, anyway. She'd already interviewed an autosexual, androsexual, omnisexual, skoliosexual, and a big brawny guy who identified as a lesbian. The piece received backlash, as Clo did her trademark bitchy editorializing, causing some of the participants to feel disrespected and tricked. The minor scandal, however, won

Clorinda another celebrity client whom she's been dressing for events ever since.

On screen: an image of one of Bellmer's dolls wearing a garment by Vivienne. A steel-hooped cage crinoline, naked. Tumorous protuberances and shiny rolls visible through the see-through exoskeleton. The crinoline extends the doll—making the form even more odd. Several intestine-shaped boas with real bird feathers and human hair wrap around the doll's torso. The next image is the same, but between the doll's body and the crinoline are miniature figurines of a dog and a horse, trapped. In the following image, the third in this series, the crinoline is covered in a layer of silk, those animals no longer visible. The doll is at rest—shrouded in silk privacy, almost elegant.

Lars feels he's leaking—eyes and cock and pores. He looks out the window and focuses on the bodega light in the distance which streams magenta and green diagonally across the street, eyes burning. He pauses the video and studies the sculpture, recalling a warning issued by medieval mystic Marguerite Porete at the start of *The Mirror of Simple Souls*:

> **Theologians and other clerks, You**
> **won't understand this book—**
> **However bright your wits— If you do**
> **not meet it humbly. And in this way,**
> **Love and Faith Make you surmount**
> **Reason, for They are the protectors of**
> **Reason's house.**

Resting his hand on his tight stomach, he wants to meet Vivienne's work humbly, with Love and Faith, as he recalls that it's been a while since his last colonic. He needs to get his gut bacteria back on track, as he's been craving fast food, pies, and other standard American stuff, dense and salty and sweet. In addition to spin classes, lifting, and saunas, Lars keeps a clean diet, mainly subsisting on plates of fish, eggs, greens, and the occasional complex carbohydrate. A formerly chubby kid, he prefers to feel purified and a little hungry at all times. The hollowness keeps him focused, for the most part, and avoiding weight gain and boosting the visibility and reputation of the gallery have been his two consistent goals. And more recently: growing a simple soul.

The soul will be for both himself and the gallery, which have fused into one dented entity. Typically, he's able to stay on the path—disciplined, rigorous, ambitious. Once in a while, however, his mind-body betrays him and he binges. It was after a sugar binge that Lars was forced to confront the rotten state of his own soul. (His own soul, like a sad calorie.) On Halloween, his neighbors had gone out for the night, leaving a giant bowl of peanut butter cups in the hallway for the neighborhood kids. Lars intended to take two pieces but ended up eating the whole bowl, leaving nothing for the children. He'd stopped counting after forty. The next day, he sweated through two hot yoga classes, started a three-day juice cleanse, and purchased Maguerite Porete's *The Mirror of Simple Souls*, which he saw in the window of a used bookstore downtown and took to be a sign. That was a month and a half ago.

A small poem by Vivienne Volker about sex and horses (Lars guesses) is playing on the YouTube video right now, words moving vertically. His eyes are closing and the only light in the gallery is the one emanating from his screen—spitting red, white, and pink hues onto his black clothes. From above, he appears small and slumped in his swivel chair as an image of Velour as a toddler appears. He dreams he's galloping, a horse into the woods, and the woods are lined with pies and the dismembered corpses of humans and dolls. He can't tell plastic from flesh from pie crust. The comments flare. Lars sleeps.

Beautiful poem!
complicit in the surrealist's sickening pedophilia
good riddance
why not show a more relevant artist

Mesmerizing
taken to another world
kidnapped
thank you for making this, Eda Singer, bless xx
WHORE

~

From the street, Lars is a smudge against the blue rectangle of his computer, his head bald and shining neath art light. He began the meditative
ritual of shaving it a few years ago when his hairline started seriously
vanishing around his thirty-third birthday. His booted feet are up on the
desk twitching as the street lights switch from green to yellow to red. The
homeless man, crumpled red umbrella under his arm, uses the gallery
window as a mirror while he gestures over and over again the application
of lipstick to his chapped open mouth. He walks backward into the street,
eyeing Lars. On screen, lines from Vivienne's 1977 collection *The Machine-
Gunneress in a State of Grace* appear then recede:

I WAS A SERIOUS TRICK
MASKED AND GALLOPING
IN MAGENTA VISCOSE
AROUND THE THINNING RING
Fabric through which the stars
Shot into a zone roofless
The light which ate and made me
A manic mystic
Galloping music looped
I tripped
Looking for you
In the crowded audience
As the night wore

Immense red changed to forlorn blue
A whore
Taken to another world

≈

LARS 10:28pm
i HAVE to do this show Clo
just finished watchin
THE MOST transcendent video
by some rando

CLORINDA 10:29 pm
perfect timing
i set the meeting up
Vivienne and Velour are expecting you
they said it's best to come any time
after 12pm on December 19
(after church)

LARS 10:29pm
!!

CLORINDA 10:29pm
Vivienne's Catholic
not sure if she's for real

LARS 10:29pm
are you coming with me?

CLORINDA 10:29pm
better if you go solo
i have to dress Mark for a dinner

LARS 10:30pm
are they taking other meetings?

CLORINDA 10:30pm
doubt it
Vel seemed calm
shell shocked idk

LARS 10:30pm
good
I FEEL ALTERED

CLORINDA 10:30pm
yeah, soul searching?
they are waiting for you
i sung your praises
Velour had heard your name

LARS 10:30pm
fuck yeah

CLORINDA 10:30pm
when will you be home

LARS 10:32pm
need to research this family more
so did Vivienne convince Wilma to jump out the window?

CLORINDA 10:32pm
if i told you to jump out a window, would you?

LARS 10:32pm
fucking DUH
sweet clorindaaaaa

CLORINDA 10:32pm
can someone be CONVINCED?

LARS 10:32pm
depends ?

CLORINDA 10:32pm
if you can be CONVINCED to jump out a window
maybe you deserve whats comin

LARS 10:33pm
what do u think happens to the soul
after jumping

CLORINDA 10:33pm
it goes to the wood of suicides
if Viv agrees to do the show
you should do a publicity stunt
to keep ppl engaged

LARS 10:33pm
road of sighs
thighs
highs

CLORINDA 10:34pm
u need 2 eat

LARS 10:35pm
what kind of stunt

CLORINDA 10:35pm
simple elegant classic
like
a brick through the window

LARS 10:36pm
i like that
but i just had the glass replaced

~

When Lars wakes, the street cleaners are sweeping. The video, playing. Homeless guy, sleeping. Lars feels totally coated in the dirty-bright residue of Vivienne's thick history, as told in images on screen. His mouth is dry, eyes swelled, and his wrinkled clothes smell of sweat and old coffee. He needs to go home and change immediately.

VELOUR

December 16
Morning

After dropping Vesta off at school, Velour approaches the house like a cloud, vaporous and without essence—blank, barely moving. In the car, the child ran her mouth while double fisting waffles in the front seat and insisting that Velour pay *extra special* attention to Franz today, giving him love, because he apparently had nightmares. Vesta claimed the dog was kicking and crying in bed. Velour promised. But, she doesn't remember driving home, doesn't even know she's walking towards the door and that the door belongs to her house. She's recalling a conversation she'd overheard between her mother and Todd, one of the curators at the NAT Museum, last night. Vivienne's end went something like:

I won't
How should I know
I'm not a therapist
Wanting to include
Sure
Fine
A warning

No

No

No

Absolutely

No

Yes

I understand

The machine

I do not think

May I finish?

Would object to my being in the same show

There are many reasons I stopped

Among them, the creation of art, especially with the intention of showing to a public

Was not good for my character

Sure

Yes

Fine

By then, Hans was gone

No

Love? Amour?

Mais bien sur

Oui

Oui

I'm nearly ninety

Well, eighty-two but still

Religious

Yes

I myself don't condone suicide

God-given life

Sure, we spoke

I told her a tale of a ribbon and a road

It was a metaphor
No
No
An interrogation
C'est impossible!
No
You've already made up your mind
Yes
Okay
Right
A statement, fine
Online
Keep the works for now
I haven't seen them in years
And I don't want to see them now
Fine
Fine
Yes
They're at rest
Resting
With all due respect
Oh
Would have been
Yes
Some grace
Goodbye

Velour stumbles into the kitchen, tosses the metal wad of keys onto the table, sits in her husband's chair, and opens her laptop. As she reads the NAT's statement, declaring that they've removed Vivienne from the upcoming show, guilt needles her sides. She hadn't been listening to Vesta at all. The girl had said they were making something in school that day—something she was quite excited about, but Velour can't recall what or why—and Vesta had provided instructions—something about love, the dog, nightmares—what? He's over there—curled in a lopsided ball, looking half-traumatized. Velour chucks a waffle at his head. He flips it over with his nose, nudges it away, then slurps it up as though liquid.

Franz Kline was the death messenger. The dog informed Velour: *your husband is gone.* Franz never cared about Velour, never licked or pawed her gently awake. They were suspicious of one another. At best, they coexisted. In truth, Velour found the dog ugly and smug, his splotchy hair and skinny legs, brown with stripes of warm black and a red undertone which makes him look, in this winter light, like an oily otter. She eyes the tired creature, lighting a cigarette, thinking back to that other December morning, when Franz pressed his cold wet nose against the back of her sleeping hand, waking her up. As she walked downstairs, Velour sensed the end.

Why hadn't Franz intervened? Velour had heard stories of dogs rescuing humans from varieties of danger. If Franz had only been a better, smarter dog . . . her mind wanders into the white clouds around the house as the snow melts. She lies down on the floor beside him. *What are you looking at?* she whispers, as the dog, who looks ferocious up-close, smooshes his face against hers. Stunned at the sudden affection, she springs to her feet, nearly collapsing.

Velour goes upstairs to check on Vivienne, whom she hasn't seen all morning. She opens the door without knocking, forgetting it's Thursday and Lou has off. When she busts in, he's sitting up in bed, bare chested and staring, and Vivienne's beside him, dead asleep. There's a tenderness that moves between their resting bodies which Velour hardens against. Curled into a small fetal ball, her mother looks like a child. Velour's heart quickens.

-Uh. What's up? Lou whispers.

-Just checking on you guys.

-Why?

-I had a weird . . . a weird feeling, Velour whispers. For a second, she mistakes her own voice for her daughter's.

-One of your *feelings* huh?

-Shut up.

-Are you gonna keep standing there? Lou whispers.

-No. Can you go to the patriot grocery today?

-Sure. I have some shit to do in town anyway.

Vivienne stirs and Lou keeps staring at Velour in that particularly pene-
trating, stuporous manner. She reverses out of the room, awkward—like an
animal or an alien, a notch or two away from human. Velour and Lou refer
to the big store at the edge of town as the patriot grocery because they play
songs about America and there's a giant painting of a flag on the front windows. She can't think of what they would need there, but Velour doesn't
want Lou around. She has to focus. To focus, she needs to sit in Max's
chair at the kitchen table, where she can feel her body getting enlivened
by extra shots of electricity and druggy euphoria. Velour sees the chair as a
power center. The other power center is the basement where they keep her
father's doll sculpture, *The Machine-Gunneress in a State of Grace*.

In the chair, she starts her day's work. She begins looking through
the hundreds of photos on her computer, clicking on images of her mother's drawings and sculptures and life while occasionally flashing to Max,
his skinny body slumped over the white farm table. Velour herself had
never shot up. Perhaps, she thinks, looking at the pictures, her aversion
to needles has something to do with growing up around tools for sewing
and seam ripping, instruments which change the form of anything. The
silvery alchemical vigor of needles—mend, kill, cure, poison, rip.

Alterations, alterations.

~

Onscreen: Velour and Vivienne in an apartment in Berlin, late 1970s, with
a sea green interior. This was taken around the time Delia, an eccentric
friend of her mother's, had shown Velour pictures of the artwork created

by Hans and Vivienne when they were together. Little Velour, probably four, was ecstatic, for she'd finally get to peer inside the souls of those who made her, as her mother refrained from talking about that older, unholier portion of her life. Delia called her Vel Bel and Velour abhorred the rhymey nickname, correcting the obnoxious woman each time.

When Velour asked Delia why her father did such terrible things to those dolls, Delia shrugged and said perhaps he was sad. But Velour was sure the opposite must be true: those dolls *made* him—made him sad. Once, Velour shoved a pencil through her own baby doll's eye and afterwards, startled that she could commit such an act, cried and cried. When Delia showed the young Velour a drawing her mother made featuring a girl about to get impaled by a sewing needle, body lying flat as a piece of fabric, Velour screamed. *Mein Liebling, Mein Liebling*, Delia replied. In that same apartment, Velour watched Delia pose for an artist named Jerrold while her mother was working. She watched Delia's face and body miraculously change sizes and shapes, staying stone-still then moving, anticipating Jerrold's moods. It was hard work, Velour concluded, being a muse.

Once, Jerrold painted Velour while she looked through drawings on the floor. When he asked her to take her clothes off, she threw a book at his face. Jerrold Urn was handsome and blonde and icy, like an actor playing the part of an artist. Years later, she ran into him at a club downtown and they made slow, passionate love in the bathroom, their bodies twisting around the toilet. He was uglier by then, which made him more attractive. After his death in the noughties, he became famous for his "Delia Series," which shows Delia Durant in various poses. Sometimes, she is part animal: dog or horse or bird. One of the paintings in the Delia series features young Velour reading in the corner. Her face is not her own, but the grown-up countenance of Delia Durant. Her body is totally naked and she has wings. The wings are an angel's or a bird's.

～

Lou's weighty, metallic footsteps shake the ceiling and Velour holds her breath as she anticipates his arrival in the kitchen. She taps her foot against the table until he appears.

-What're you doing *now*? He asks.

-Nothing.

-Can I see the *nothing*?

-No.

She slams the machine shut.

-You're nuts.

-I'm working on something. Don't worry about it.

Lou sits down next to her, rests his chin on his hand, leans closer, too close. He wears a silver ring on his middle finger with a ball bearing. She reaches out and touches the little metal balls, spinning it around and around, surprising herself. He doesn't even flinch—so steady, unflappable, that she wonders, as she strokes the metal, what *would* throw him off. She moves away.

-Can you go to the grocery store. Or upstairs. Or the basement. *Somewhere.*

-You're sending me to the basement? Lou asks, crossing his arms.

-I need quiet. To work on this thing. Is Mom still sleeping?

-Yeah. I don't think she wants to wake up.

-Today or ever?

-Today. *Today.*

-Are you going to read it? Velour asks.

-The museum's statement? I read it, Velour. Of course I did. You think I'm illiterate.

-It's like she's volunteering for it, Velour says.

-For what?

-I don't know. Deletion.

-*Deletion,* Lou repeats, nodding his head.

-What do you think? Velour asks.

-She's kind of like a saint. Or maybe just a boomer. She *gets* that the internet isn't real.

-The internet *is* real. And she's not a boomer, Lou. She's older than that. See, I knew this would happen. Now, we're having a conversation. And I'm trying to *do* something.

-*Is* this a conversation? I'm *leaving*, okay.

-How long will you be gone?

-All fucking day.

Today, the world's mutable—people melting into other people, voices joining—those silver ball bearings circling slow around his dense, pinkish finger. Even now, as Lou walks toward the door, he's also Jerrold Urn—what he could have looked and moved like during the gap—the years between when he painted Velour and followed her into the bathroom. Her heart is pounding and her uterus is cramping as she watches Lou-Jerrold drive away.

Velour feels Lou to be one of her only true connections to the town she lives in, as his family has been here for generations. Occasionally, he speaks of the way it used to be, which makes Velour, by association, more permanent—real. It was all farmland and woods and one factory and when he was in high school, just one movie theater, one gas station, two small markets. To Lou, it's full. Lou was a regional baseball star in high school. After graduation, he worked at a small factory two towns north where he dipped bats in paint. After a while, he just wanted to be outside. Velour opens her computer, looks at her own blurry reflection in the smudged screen, and continues.

～

In this photo, Vivienne is holding Velour. In this one, Vivienne is sewing, surrounded by drawings. Vivienne is threading the needle's eye. The entrance to heaven is impossibly narrow. Very few souls are simple and lean enough to fit. On the contrary, hell and its thresholds are everywhere.

One can stumble upon it, fall in. Goodbye. Velour counts. Thus far, she's compiled ninety-six images.

She pulls up her father's self-portrait, the one dated 1971, completed while living with Vivienne. Velour studies this one often and she's written a forty-page piece on it, unpublished and sitting in her computer like the rest of her writings. She's begun to see herself in his arched eyebrow and incensed nostril, her body bent and tucked into his hairline. A mad clown with voltaic lines shooting outward to form a harlequin collar, that soft fence around his neck. She loves him, she thinks. She used to speak about these things with Max. Now, she speaks them into the air around his chair. She says aloud the name of her father. Franz barks and Velour jumps. She gets up and makes a sudden lunging motion at the dog, who backs up. *What?* You *should* be scared of me. He hangs his head. She lays down on the kitchen floor beside him and he shakes a little, then moves toward her as though all is forgotten, like he's convulsed the threat right out of his body. She takes Franz's snout in her hand and kisses it. He shakes, then curls up at her side.

Beauty will be convulsive or will not be at all, said Breton. Velour has hundreds—maybe thousands of pages of notes with quotes like that one—arty slogans and bombastic declarations alongside essays and poems and sketches fueled by works by her parents and other Surrealists. As she lies on the black and white tiled floor staring up at the white ceiling—Velour thinks of these phrases and her cloudful of words and pictures, attempts to trace lines in order to understand where she came from and thus—where she might wind up—her entrails and ends—how they'd eventually dissolve into hot flat desert—light without image above a road without end. At the end of a family tree—no more thought. Just equilibrium, rest. She can almost see through the ceiling, right into the room where her mother is sleeping. Or maybe she's dead. She inhales, closes her eyes, opens her mouth wide, and lets the air out. The thought brings sudden peace. *Or maybe she's dead.*

When Velour wakes up, she's still on the floor next to the dog. It's nearly noon. She runs to the bathroom and Franz follows. Her urine is pinkish red and when she wipes, there's a red line with jelly-like clots. Her period's here early. When she stands up, her phone falls out of her pocket, lit with a text message which she reads as blood drips onto the floor.

CLORINDA SALAZAR 11:51 am
heard what happened
OBSCENE
HOW IS SHE HOLDING UP
SHE IS A TOTAL. FUCKING. WARRIOR.
wilma needed ZERO help from your mother
or anyone else with that window business
how UNFEMINIST to assume she did!

has Vivienne found another place to show her work?
i ask because Lars is a lifelong
fan of your mom and thinks its an utter crime
against humanity that the NAT threw her out like trash
TOTAL confidence that Lars
will treat both Viv (LOVE
HER) and her IMPORTANT GROUNDBREAKING work
with utmost care and respect
the gallery is empty right now
seems to be waiting for Vivienne
would your mother be willing to take a meeting
with Lars (Arden) and consider doing a solo show
at Gallery X in the VERY NEAR future?
lmk when u have a sec
xClo

The phone goes dark. Velour will deal with Clorinda later. After wiping the blood off the bathroom floor, she examines the gelatinous globs in the toilet, like wet gummy candies. She reaches in and grabs one, presses down and tries to crush it. Holding the dripping specimen, she feels, for an instant, that it's a piece of art she's made. She places the clot on her tongue like communion, tastes iron and salt, then opens her mouth and lets it fall back into the toilet. She's chalk-white, all the vibrancy from her face draining, clumping, and getting squeezed out of her and into the sewer.

In the kitchen, she slides on her green winter boots and opens the side door. Sore, she watches Franz as he jumps around the last patches of snow vanishing into black puddles of muddy nothing.

-No! No! No!

She yells at the dog who is charging a trio of white, mud-splattered ducks wobbling along the edge of the yard. The ducks belong to a stone farmhouse up the street situated on the wooded route outside the new neighborhood of mansions. They move up and down like awkward ground clouds as Velour runs to the corner where her yard turns into the field. Franz happily gallops in circles around Velour and the birds, herding them into a pile, obeying the order not to kill. She tucks one of the mud-caked ducks under her arm, suddenly moved by how peaceful the bird seems as it leans feathered weight into her, its quick heart beating on her ribs. Like Vesta as a baby, she carries the creature toward the edge of the yard.

Velour can feel how much easy damage she could do, its skinny neck in her hand. She squeezes, looking into the black diamond eyes before releasing. Something gets passed back and forth between her and the bird—energy, aura, memory—as she strokes its slick white coat. A shiny black pickup approaches, slowing down outside her home. All three ducks quack and Velour's body vibrates as blood drips down her inner thigh. Mac Wallace steps out wearing a suit and tie. She can already smell him—his car's tree-shaped Black Ice air freshener, civet, cologne.

-Mac, hi.

-These aren't *your* ducks, are they? He asks.

-They're visiting.

Mac points to the LOST DOG sign and Velour winces as muscles pulp her uterus.

-Got a call from somebody who said they saw Pepper running around here. Wondering if you saw anything.

-No.

Her stomach relaxes as Mac reaches for the bird, touching her gently with the back of his large hand.

-Mackenzie and Lisa are messed up about Pep.

-I'm sure, Velour says, nodding.

-I always thought I was gonna be one of those guys with a big dog. More like Franz, or even bigger, you know? A dog people would be afraid of.

Franz is nuzzling the tail feathers, crying a little. Velour shoves him off.

-Instead, I end up with a four-pound chihuahua, Mac says, half-laughing. And I miss the fucker. I really do.

-Of course you do, says Velour.

-Give us a call, will you? If you see her?

Mac walks backward to his truck. He's broad with big tan hands, the type of man Velour is continually surprised to see wearing a suit and tie. Her body flushes as he loosen the tie, disappearing into the front seat. She waves back, feeling idiotic. She squeezes the duck as her body discharges another bloody clump. With her free hand, she reaches down and grabs it. She shows the clump to the duck, then tosses it, watching as it melts into the mud.

As Mac pulls away, he watches Velour float around the yard in her white robe, one duck quacking under her arm as two others trail behind, the dog circling the bonkers flock. He watches as she tosses something into the landscape, which makes him feel queasy and high. Almost happy. Not quite. Velour Bellmer must be, he thinks, the strangest woman he's ever seen. Known her for years. Never gets familiar. All day, Velour and those fucking ducks will be roving around his mind rent free. As he imagines him and Velour passing a duck back and forth between them over the wet yard, he turns the music up and takes his tie off, driving fast back to his neighborhood, The Residenz, for lunch. He tries to shake the image off.

~

In the kitchen, Velour fishes her phone from the pocket of her robe and reads Clorinda's text again. She types LARS ARDEN into the search box and widens his internet picture: a man with a shaved head walking down the street dressed in drapey black clothing beneath the headline GALLERIST LARS ARDEN ON HIS SIMPLE STREET STYLE. There's a *cleanness* about him which brings into relief her current grittiness— covered in period gore, duck, mud. Looking at the image, she feels she should shower. He's wearing black loafers without socks and a gargoyle ring on his pinky. Velour enlarges his hand—much smaller than Mac Wallace's. Then, she zooms in on his eyes: gray and glassy with yellow lines.

"The city is total insanity," explains Arden, "so I dress to stay grounded. I wear black. I have a uniform. But I add flash . . ."

Her mother calls out from above: *Velour? Vel? Velour!* Ambling up the stairs, tripping over her robe halfway, shaky—another clot of blood. She needs a cigarette. Maybe food. She can't remember if she's eaten. Velour sits on the edge of her mother's bed.

-Don't get old, Vivienne says.

-What's the problem?

-My body. I don't recognize it.

-You're fine. Don't be dramatic.

-It's past noon! I slept past noon. That's not *fine*.

-Well, yesterday you got bad news. So, it makes sense.

-Darling, darling, wow. You look like shit too.

-Thanks.

-I *need* to go to church.

-Didn't you *just* go?

-Yes. You're quite pale, Vel.

-Do you want to do a show?

-Do you *see that*? Vivienne asks, pointing.

-What?

-There's a light. Near the door! There!

-This again?

-Just a small one this time.

-Do you want to do a show?

-I've been booted from the show, remember?

-A different show. Solo. Only you.

-There it is. The light. I need to get to church, Vel Bel.

Vivienne is sprawled out, body like a kinked X on the bed. Velour gets up and walks over to the window. The ducks are on the move, tottering homeward.

-Don't call me that, please. I doubt there's Mass today. The show . . . the solo show, Velour continues.

-I need to be in an enclosed space. I feel exposed.

-Remember Salazar? Velour asks.

-Mediocre painter. Threw his wife from a window, Vivienne says.

-Let me *finish*, Velour says.

-Can you drive me to church? Vivienne asks.

-Salazar's wife said she *fell*, Velour says.

-They never really *fall*, Vivienne scoffs.

-Either way, his daughter Clorinda . . .

-So you'll drop me at church?

-Let me finish.

-Go on, darling.

-Clorinda is an old friend of mine. Her boyfriend, Lars Arden, owns a gallery. He wants to show your work in his space. She stares at her mother, who looks many years younger when lying down. For a second, wrinkles smoothed, she looks like a combination of Hans Bellmer and Velour, like Vivienne is *their* offspring.

-The light! It's back. Bigger. Over there, Vivienne says, pointing.

-It's a migraine, Mom. Do you want meds? What about the show?

-Must we medicalize *everything*?

-Okay. It's *mystical*.

Velour snaps her fingers in front of Vivienne's eyes.

-The rapture of Saint Teresa. Saint Paul's vision on the road.

-What?

-Mystical visions which some lunatics ascribe to medical issues.

-Right. But you're not Saint Teresa.

-Solo show, solo show, Vivienne mutters under her breath.

-I know a solo show *pales* in comparison to conversions and angelic raptures, but it could be good for you. It would happen very soon, I think. He's young and energetic. But, it's up to you.

-*Young and energetic?* Who? Vivienne asks.

-The gallerist. Are you still with me? Velour asks.

Velour, oozing blood, squeezes her thighs together.

-I saw something.

-The light?

-*In* the light.

-What did you see?

-The show, Vivienne mutters, eyes wide.

-Yes or no? Velour asks.

-I'd like to meet this character first. Lars, right? Have him come here.

-I'll work on it.

-I know they're saying things about me, Vivienne says.

≈

For the moment, all is settled.

Equilibrium.

End.

Vivienne is upstairs eating and Franz, damp and panting on the cold floor.

Lou: gone. Vesta: school.

Everyone: living and absent.

Good.

She sits down in her husband's chair and begins making the images she's compiled into a video. Her period, for the moment, has ceased. She convulses a little, stomach spasming. She can feel Max moving through her as she becomes a medium, automaton. Finally focused—here and gone, she writes a biography of her mother in a detached but admiring tone inspired by one of the fan letters Vivienne received when Velour was a girl. Velour had found it in a drawer and read the words over and over while her mother, in the other room, worked her Singer sewing machine. Velour sets the one-hundred and three images to music—an electronic mix she made with Max during their MDMA phase, slowed down and remixed, with noises he recorded around their yard and the field, for atmosphere. She creates a burner account on YouTube, using the first name that springs to mind: Eda Singer. The music plays.

An enchantment.

More blood.

A clown dressed like her father hovers above a table, an erect cock shooting from its smooth exterior and dripping something—blood, paint, semen. Chairs are flipped upside-down on the table like someone's about to clean. And a woman sits alone covered in bird feathers, a beak for a mouth. She runs her wings over the surface. If you looked into the window at Velour from the tree with the LOST DOG sign, you might see a mound of white muddy fabric slumped over a flat silver brick, a few stray feathers falling upon her like snow. The sun is low, only a few days away from the year's darkest day, which Velour looks forward to. The day the sun stops.

∼

When Velour wakes for the third time today, she's face down on her computer and someone with a familiar scent, close and drone-like, pushes hot breath onto her neck. She inhales and groans, spreading her legs. How much has she had to drink today? To eat? She can't recall how many cigarettes, nor how much extra love, if any, she has given Franz, per her daughter's morning request—a request which must have expired by now. She thinks of Mac, his leather interior and musky cologne, smooth and hard beside her bloody lawn and lost ducks. Once, she sat in Mac's black truck—she felt held, upright, and cool—like a high school girl in an older guy's ride, the landscape a thrilling mix of there and not. But it's not Mac behind her. Neither is it Lars, the man in the images.

It's Lou.

-Fuck, she whispers, blinking.
-Is that your dad? asks Lou, pointing to Hans Bellmer's mad clown self-portrait, still enlarged on her screen.
-That's Dad, Velour says.
-Makes sense that he made you.
-He made *that*, too.

Velour points to a 1963 drawing by Bellmer which hangs framed on the kitchen's backwall: human cocks affixed to tables and asses pointed up.

-I know.

Lou doesn't move. He's too close to see, so she looks down at the shiny white table and traces the chipped flowers embellishing the corners. They're no longer flowers. How long had she been asleep?

-Mom never hung any art in our house.

-My mom never hung any art in our house, either.

Finally, he moves away from Velour and begins putting the groceries away. Simple bright colors—red, blue, yellow, move from his hands into the refrigerator and cabinets, disappearing. Velour closes her laptop, clips her hair up higher and smiles, soothed by his easy kitchen maneuvers. She rubs her eyes and in her fuzzy state, desires to tell him everything about her childhood.

-Mom demanded I take that one down when she moved in, Velour says, pointing to the drawing of penis tables. She rests her face against the cool porcelain table and sighs.

-But you didn't listen.

-Do you think it's any good? Velour asks.

-The drawing? Sure. Not as . . . affecting . . . as the thing in the basement, Lou says, clutching a gallon of milk. He pours a cup of coffee and places it on the table before her. She takes a sip and burns her mouth. Velour can hear Vivienne on the stairs, making her descent at the usual snail's pace. She spots her mother's platform boots below the edge of her long black coat.

-I saw an old friend from high school at the grocery store, says Lou.

-Wait! What time is it? Velour gasps.

-3:11.

-Vesta!

Velour bolts to the door.

-What's happening? Vivienne yells from the stairs.

-We're going to pick up Vesta, Lou says.

-I'm coming with you! You can drop me at church.

-Jesus Christ. Hurry up!

Lou gets into the driver's seat of the PT Cruiser as Velour leashes up Franz, her mouth still burning. Vivienne slides into the front seat while Velour and Franz wait in the back, Velour tapping her foot. Lou, adjusting the mirror, looks at Velour and Velour looks down, then pinches her cheeks and slaps her own face.

-Why slap yourself? *Why?* Vivienne asks.

-I need to *wake up.*

-Consider changing your clothes, Vivienne says.

-The school moms already think I'm *unfit*. Now I forget to pick her up. They'll have a field day.

-You're fit, Lou says.

-Just *drive!*

They shoot through the cornfield-lined backroads to the elementary school. The muddy ducks are waddling in a line, almost home, and Velour can feel the dried blood on her thighs cracking in the cold. Vivienne beams at Lou, grabbing his hand. Everyone's smoking, windows open. The car is freezing and Franz is splayed on Velour's lap like a blanket, his hair shedding, swirling around the backseat. *Stop,* she whispers. She wants something to stop, but she's not sure what. The constant movement of the car. Franz's creaturely breathing. She exhales into fast motion dead grasses. Since that first time she and Max drove through, she knew these roads would be an antidote. But there are poisons, too. Where, for instance, did the last ten years of her life go?

Velour leans her head against the window, trancing into the flickering field.

There.

They went there.

There.

There.

And there.

She lets her forehead knock against the glass.

-This'll be my last smoke of the day, declares Vivienne from the front.

-Were you smoking in bed this morning? Velour snaps.

-She doesn't usually, Lou says.

-Don't defend her. That's *my* house. And I don't want any disasters.

-Relax, darling. My fate is not Ingeborg's. I *know* I won't die by fire.

-Ingeborg? Lou asks.

-An Austrian writer, mutters Velour.

-Died by fire in Rome. Asleep with cigarette, says Vivienne.

-*I'm writing with my burnt hand about the nature of fire,* she once wrote, says Velour.

-Very good, darling, Vivienne whispers.

-You fucking people, says Lou, shaking his head.

Lou ups the volume on the droning electronica and they roll into the empty lot.

-*There's* my little girl. See, she's *fine!* Vivienne says.

In her Vivienne coat, puff sleeves and custom buttons, sitting on the concrete steps, Vesta looks like a drawing of a girl, the building towering tenuously above her, threatening to topple. Velour begins to cry—quiet and without tears. Franz and Vesta stand up at the same time, Franz in the backseat and Vesta on the steps, and the girl runs to the car, throwing herself into the backseat, hugging the dog. She glares at Velour, eyebrows squiggling into terror. Velour anticipates her daughter's question, which makes her feel like a mother for a second.

-No. *Nothing* bad happened. We're late because I'm stupid. But *there's no bad news,* okay? We're gonna drop Nana off at church now.

Vesta's face smooths into a smile.

-I *knew* you'd come.

-Yeah? Good.

-Did you give Franz love? Vesta asks, stroking the dog.

-Definitely.

-Are all the girls at school jealous of your coat? asks Vivienne.

-Um, not really. Vesta shakes her head, wiggling out of her backpack.

-Did they find Pepper yet? Vesta asks.

-No, Lou says.

-Can I have a drag? Vesta asks Vivienne.

-No you may *not*, says Velour.

-Nana said if you only take a few puffs a week, it's not bad.

-Isn't it a mortal sin to give a child drugs?

-A few puffs? Maybe a venial sin, Vivienne says.

-What's *venial?* asks Vesta.

-A level down from the *really* bad ones, Vivienne says.

-God doesn't mind as much?

-Venial sin does not deprive the sinner of sanctifying grace, friendship with God, charity, and consequently, eternal happiness, Vivienne says, robotic and dreamy.

-What's that from? asks Lou.

-The Catechism of the Catholic Church, she says, ashing out the window, beaming.

-You're ridiculous, Velour says.

-You're not *ridiculous*, Vesta says.

-Thank you, darling. After Hans, I found God, Vivienne says, stroking Lou's hand.

-I know, he says.

-Grandpa was a *genius*, declares Vesta.

-In a way, Vivienne says.

-Is God a genius?

-What do you think? Vivienne asks, turning around to face Vesta.

-I think *yes*. Can I get my nails done? Vesta asks.

-For the last time: *no*. Stop terrorizing me, Velour says.

Lou laughs.

-Why can't she get her nails done? he asks.

-Cause she's too young. Why do you care?

-Mackenzie gets *hers* done, Vesta says.

-Mackenzie's mom is a pushover.

-Lisa? That family has good trash.

Mackenzie Wallace, the daughter of Mac and Lisa and the companion of Pepper the chihuahua, is in Vesta's class. As far as Velour can tell, the girls are sometimes friends, depending on their erratic moods. The Wallace family lives on a nearby hill at the very top of a neighborhood of McMansions called The Residenz, its streets named after German castles: Mespelbrunn Avenue, Wartburg Court, Colditz Circle, Heidelberg Hill. When Pepper went missing last week, the family plastered the area with Lost Dog signs.

-Like what? Tell me, Velour says.

-Gameboys. Bikes. CDs.

-Mackenzie has diamonds on her nails, Vesta says.

Franz barks.

-What's his problem? Velour asks Vesta.

-Franz, what's wrong?! cries Vesta.

-He's barking at *me*! Velour says.

Velour locks eyes with the dog and he gives her a hard stare.

-I don't think you loved him today. He's mad now.

-Maybe he's hungry, Lou says.

-It's like he doesn't know me, says Velour, squirming away.

-He's just *communicating*. Dogs bark, Lou says.

Vesta buries her head in Franz's fur.

-You didn't *love* him! Vesta repeats, voice muffled.

-Jesus Christ. Lou, testify to my love.

-She loved him. Dogs feel our energy. They're like sponges, Lou offers.

-I *know* that, Velour snaps.

-Ah, here we are. *His* house, Vivienne says as they pull up to the church. She groans.

-What's wrong, babe? asks Lou.

-My legs hurt. They're heavy, like I'm undergoing purgatorial punishment.

Velour rolls her eyes, then studies Lou, who appears genuinely concerned about Vivienne's legs. The dog quits barking and for a moment, all's quiet. Velour has always found the church plain for a Catholic place: a stone A-frame with some stained glass windows and a brown roof with a skinny white wooden cross stuck into the top, like a medieval birthday cake. Behind the church sits a hill and a graveyard whose headstones date back to the eighteenth century. Many of the names rubbed out by time. And so many babies. When they first moved here, she'd walk around the graveyard with Max and they'd linger over a headstone near the front—oxidation-green and cradle-shaped. The name faded with time but the date remained: 1808.

Max Furio's body rests in one of the back rows with the newer stones. Velour rarely goes. He's not in the graveyard. He's home. And he wasn't exactly a believer—save for ghosts. He had a melancholic and heavy disposition which would suddenly shimmer, manic and twitchy. Velour can still feel his foot shaking back and forth beneath the table, quivering into her shin.

When she was a little girl, her mother often quoted Pascal: *kneel and you shall believe*, or some such thing. There were moments when Vivienne seemed to genuinely believe. The rest of the time, Velour felt her mother's religiosity was a performance or neurological ailment, an elaborate gothic cathedral from which she'd emerge someday, dazed.

-I'm going with Nana, Vesta declares, squirming out of the car after squeezing Franz.

The girl gives Velour a dirty look and grabs her grandmother's hand as they walk up the stairs. Velour gets in the front seat, huffing, and as Lou and Velour pull away, Vesta and Vivienne look like twins, buoyant in matching black, pushing past the church's stony exterior.

Velour rolls the window all the way down and closes her eyes, freezing breeze damp and cutting against her face, which feels leathery and old today. When she opens her eyes: beige fields, neutral and flat and suddenly placeless. Powerful and focused at the wheel, Lou drives fast and Velour remembers how capable he is. Watches his hands grip and turn the wheel and his groaning joins with the sound of the engine. She puts her hand on his thigh, his muscle tensing, then turns back and locks eyes with Franz, who appears flummoxed, dense jowly head cocked to one side. Velour ashes and exhales, shakes her shoulders, batting everyone's energy away. When she gets home, she needs to finish her project. Needs to focus. And she only wants Max there. They drive in silence past the orchard, gas station, half-demolished building, barn with four white hex signs—*Wilkum Wilkum Wilkum Wilkommen*—and her house rises, a smudge over the horizon.

CHURCH

-Don't let go of my hand, okay? Look at me wobble. My legs are still heavy, Vivienne says as they walk into the front room.

When Vesta steps into the church, Vivienne pulls her back, and they stay in the narthex for a while, looking at the empty pews until Vivienne catches her breath. With the crucifix looming in the distance— high, baroque, gross—Vesta feels that they're both guests, their bodies changed by the building, remade into the exact same size. Her eyes trace the contours of the hanging Christ: sinews, injuries, rags, skinny feet, crown of thorns. Vivienne releases Vesta's hand and dips her fingers into a small silver bowl of holy water, crossing herself, then spritzing some of the liquid onto her face and dabbing, rubbing it in, as though applying makeup. Vesta does the same, inhaling the cool, old, incense-dense air of the church.

Vesta's been to *His house* many times, has seen the people walking down these aisles, genuflecting, standing, kneeling, opening mouths wide for communion after uttering *Amen Amen Amen* when the priest says *Body of Christ* as he holds up a gold chalice, singing and ringing bells while wafers gets changed into flesh. Vesta's favorite part: *the mystery of faith.*

Like magic. At Mass, when the priests sing or speak, she watches her grandmother mouth the words from her seat. Still, this is the first time Vesta has been here after-hours and she feels special—granted entrance into the divine room, its blue, red, and orange stained glass windows facing the graveyard and parking lot. She can almost see her dad's headstone from here. *Beloved Father Husband Son.*

They walk down the aisle and sit in the front row. Vivienne likes to have a good seat, even when there's no show. Vesta imitates her grandmother, who never rests her body against the pew when kneeling, no matter how tired. Now, as always, her back is perfectly straight, hands together in prayer, head bowed, eyes closed tight as though thinking very hard. Vesta blinks up at Jesus's muscular and lacerated body, one of his legs crossed over the other. She focuses on the part where his foot's nailed to the wood, staring at the patch of blood until all else blurs. Vivienne's voice snaps her back into the room.

-Were you frightened?

-No. When?

-When we were late picking you up from school today.

-No. Just annoyed at Mom.

-Don't be too hard on her, V.

Vivienne closes her eyes again and bows her head. Vesta does the same. She prays that Franz is okay, and apologizes for leaving him all alone with her mother and Lou. She prays for Pepper the lost dog and for her friends at school and her whole family, too. Prays that her dad can see her right now. Her prayer, the one she repeats in her bed and in here: *let no one die anytime soon, let there be no bad news.* When she runs out of things to pray about, she prays that her mother will allow her to get her nails done. The sun is already setting over the hill and her mind wanders into the graveyard, towards her father's stone, wondering if her grandmother will be buried out there too. Shakes the thought off, wincing as she leans back against the pew, resting her head on her grandmother's bony shoulder.

-What are you praying about now? she asks.

-Act of Contrition.

-What's that?

-It's like an apology. For sins. You know that, don't you?

-What sins?

-Oh, all of them. But we're all guilty, you know.

-Did you do what they say you did?

Vivienne opens her eyes and looks up at the crucifix, squints. Seems to be turning something over and over in her mind as Vesta's insides shake and creak. It's like her stomach's a cage and Franz is in there—tossing and groaning inside the lining—muscle and fur and metal.

-I didn't push her, not literally. But that doesn't mean I'm not responsible. I'm answerable, in a sense. Not to them, the voices, mechanical . . . those . . . people talking. But to Him. To you. Myself. Another power, divine. Not them. No. But. I sensed Wilma would go and I didn't do anything to *stop her*. I was younger, much younger, Vesta. You have to understand. Not as young as *you*, but much younger than your mother is now. One room and one bathroom, everything small. Pictures—drawings—their art, all around. Cockroaches. The sewing machine that's upstairs now. But it was new then, if you can imagine *that*. When I see it, I see it small and green, a memory, like all of it could fit inside one of those glass balls—you know what I'm talking about? Snow globes. You have one, don't you? I think she wanted to go back home. I didn't know anything back then. Still don't. Love, art. These words! Maybe you'll figure them out. Your grandfather made this beautiful drawing called *The Red Embryo*. Have your mother show you on the internet sometime when I'm gone. I don't know where it is now. I was happy, in a sense. I mean, I had your grandfather. All to myself. I felt spotlit. I heard *click, click* . . . something moving in my head and all around. Light, sound. I was way too open. I don't care much about their words, all the chatter. But I care, in a sense, about what's under them. I welcome what's coming. Welcome it.

I've been at the end for a while now. Approaching. The middle of the labyrinth. My body! I mean *look* at this thing. Like a piece of eucharist getting digested, soggy soggy. I was thinking about this word *oblation*. I wanted to offer myself up. Still do. Sweet Vesta. Oh, your face! That *face*! You are too young to look so burdened. Forget everything I just said. At least for now. Okay? Promise? It'll come back to you.

Vesta nods and they sit in silence for a long time—her head still resting against Vivienne's shoulder, bone digging into skull, and Vivienne looking up at the crucifix—quiet now, after speaking in a frenzied whisper for some minutes, transfixed. After a while, the girl starts to fidget. She taps her grandmother but Vivienne's gaze is far away now, gone. An old woman enters the church. She's wearing a bright blue winter coat that makes a swishing noise and the noise and the woman sadden Vesta, who is holding back tears now. The woman is a different kind of old—not at all like her grandmother, but maybe the same age. Vesta waves her hand in front of Vivienne's face. Nothing. This has happened before. She'll wait. The little girl looks back at the old woman, now seated on the other side of the aisle near the back.

Father Regardo appears from some hidden crevice in the far corner of the building near the place parents take noisy children during church services. The priest is a handsome, thin man with black hair who's been over at the house for dinner a few times. He wears flannel shirts and plain jeans under his priestly robes and when he nods and says *hello*, Vivienne smiles and says *good afternoon, Father*, as though his presence has brought her back from the other world. He walks, hands folded, to the very back of the church, stopping to chat with the old woman. As the priest walks away, the woman takes out an ovular golden hand mirror and studies her face. She tweezes hairs from her chin, jacket rustling. Vesta cringes, but can't look away. She thinks the woman must be crazy.

-Was Wilma *crazy*? Vesta asks.

-The dolls, in the end, kept her company. After a while, she thought they were real. That they needed to be cared for completely.

-*Did* they have to be *cared for completely*?

-Not in the way she imagined. She felt your grandfather's sculptures to be *alive*.

-Is that why she died?

Vesta's stomach feels queasy and thick, like her whole torso is filling with some black gelatinous liquid.

-No, darling. It was just her time. I shouldn't be sharing this with you. On the one hand, I want to protect you, same as your mother does. On the other hand, I think you deserve to know these things.

Father Regardo floats back up the aisle, quicker this time, and Vivienne smiles wide, nodding. Vesta's never seen her grandmother look at anyone the way she looks at the priest. His teeth are bright white. They must be fake, Vesta thinks, as she wiggles her loose tooth. He disappears into the crevice and Vesta shivers.

-Can we go home soon?

-Soon.

-Why'd she think the dolls were real?

-Her mind became a sealed chamber.

Vesta nods. The black gelatinous stuff inside her belly still there, filling the cage and overtaking her organs and Franz and spreading up towards her heart, neck, hair. Her eyes fill with tears as she rubs her stomach.

Vivienne pulls her granddaughter onto her lap and rocks her back and forth like a baby.

-But, *I knew* the dolls were dolls, and the humans, humans. And then, your mother had you. And now, here we are. Now, I have to go to confession. I'll only be a few minutes. Then we can go home.

-I'll go too.

-You're too young to confess.

-Please. Please!

-Shh, okay! You can wait for me outside.

Vesta smiles. They walk to the very front of the church and Vivienne performs a graceful, dramatic bow before the crucifix. Vesta does the same, imitating her grandmother's moves as precisely as she can, feeling like a holy dancer. For the moment, en route to confession, she is happy, floaty—no more thick black jelly. No more cage. The world's lightweight.

Vivienne kneels and winks at Vesta, then closes the curtain, disappearing into the black box. The girl waits in the dark hallway just under a stained glass window, thin and arch-shaped with an image of a faceless man—an angel? Jesus?—holding a book with one hand. Another man, dressed in yellow, kneels before him inside a bright circle. The man with the book is standing on the other man's head and they're dressed in glowing clothes, the scene sliced up by the black lines of the design. A sun, stars, a bird, a boat, water—little pixels of nature and rapture—but Vesta doesn't know where the light is coming from, how the glass is shining, as it's already dark outside, right? They've been in the church for how long? There's no way to tell. She sways back and forth, studying the blue parts of the window—sky, ocean, halo—all held by Vivienne's voice. She can't make out the words, just whispers and shuffles from the box, a reverberation of her grandmother, like Vivienne is the vessel in which the whole church floats.

Stepping out of the confessional, Vivienne seems serene, her legs strong, steady. She takes long steps, walking through the church like a gazelle. They return to the first pew in silence and Vivienne kneels, saying in her head the penance Father Regardo gave her. She repeats, repeats, repeats the prayers, prayers which are usually second nature to her but turn unfamiliar, exotic. *Hail Mary. Now and at the hour of. Our death. Our Father. Trespasses. Who art in heaven.* Vesta pouts. Bunches her skirt up into a ball. Pulls at her white tights. She's starving and misses Franz. Her belly is totally empty now—no more sludge, no more churning. She's so done. Scowls at Jesus on the cross, then at her praying grandmother. When she imagines Wilma, feeding and cradling a doll before jumping out a window, Vesta feels sludge-filled again, sick. She looks back up at Jesus— skinny, slumped—like her father. For a second, she forgets his name. She is *so* hungry. *Max. Max Furio.*

Father Regardo appears and Vivienne opens her eyes. Both nod. *Father is driving us home*, she says. Vesta squeals. On the way out, the old woman in the blue winter coat eyes Vesta, then fishes her hand mirror out of her ratty maroon purse. In the chamber, Vesta can hear the clang and rabble of the bag's innards—plastic and metal makeup containers, keys. Smoke, powder, chemically berries: this must be what the old woman's life smells like. Queasy. As she turns back to the old woman, she sees a sliver of her own face reflected in the egg-shaped mirror, pink lips and white chin. Behind her, in miniature: Vivienne and Father Regardo heading for the door.

~

In the kitchen, Velour sits back down in the chair and puts her headphones on, letting the pictures infiltrate her. The doll is dismembered—legs, torso, head—then remembered in various positions on the ground and in the air, captured in multicolor strobes. Four legs with four shoes, rolled and bound, decomposed. Then, polished ball and socket and feminine aluminum with bloated stomach. Could be a portrait of Velour right now. The fragmented doll-woman-girl-machine made by Hans and known as *The Machine-Gunneress in a State of Grace*, the one in the basement, is (aside from Hans's pencil sketch of dick-stippled tables) the only piece of his that her mother smuggled with her into the future.

Velour takes stock. Vesta and Vivienne are still at church. Lou is outside, wandering or working, whatever. The sun is down. Everyone accounted for. Everyone gone. Velour hears humming under the sound of mechanical lips and zippers. She's bleeding heavily now.

While working, she intermittently watches clips from a video fed to her by the algorithm entitled "The End is Not the End: Birth After Death." The video opens with sweeping drone shots of a mid-century modern building that resembles the church, but without the cross and instead of being surrounded by gravestones and rolling hills, it's all desert: empty, tan, cracked. Velour blinks into the screen, stupefied. An angelic voice-over speaks about the beauty and spirituality of the desert, and a new program which is enrolling participants now:

> *Here at the Center for Constant Creation, our artists bring new life into the world long after their brains stop functioning . . .*

She dozes off to the velvety voice.

Wakes to the sound of Max's music accompanied by images of crinolines, pube-covered gloves for sex organs, and weird wigs for ball and socket joints shaped like pony manes. There's a cold silence in the kitchen and on the internet. She's nearly finished. She intends for the video to be a kind of hub—the first and last stop for those on a search for Vivienne. As Velour uploads the video, Vesta and Vivienne walk through the door smelling like incense. Franz rushes to their feet.

It's 9:44 p.m.

YOUR VIDEO IS LIVE!

-How'd you get home?
-Father Regardo drove. We spoke about the solo show.
-And?
-The gallerist, what's his name? Vivienne asks.
-Lars.
-Right, *Lars*, of course. Have him come here on Sunday. After church.

∼

VELOUR BELLMER 10:20pm
my mom wants to meet lars
can he come here?
sunday
church is over at noon
any time after

CLORINDA SALAZAR 10:25pm
GREAT! he'll be there
LOVE that Viv is spiritual
send address
hope everyone's doing OK
i believe this situation = destiny
remember what happened after my parents
had their window incident?
the work FINALLY got the attention it deserved

That evening, Velour falls asleep on the couch and dreams the vast expanse of desert, ground cracking. She can almost hear Vesta grinding her teeth up above. The doll downstairs, held together by machine-like joints, has a smooth, eyeless head, cleaved like an ass. Words from one of her mother's poems play in her head:

> *Immense red changed to forlorn blue*
> *A whore*
> *Taken to another world*
>
> *An old woman*
> *In a red embryo*

She wakes a few hours before sunrise, her mouth open and dry. Where is she? On the couch, leaking cells and minerals. She can hear Max's music, the music she set the video to, fluttering in the zone over her head.

The wallpaper watches her and creaking noises emanate from the basement. Velour looks down at her dirty white robe. She'll change her clothes after she goes downstairs to see about the noise. She pushes herself up.

VIVIENNE & LOU

December 17

4:00 a.m.

She sits in bed flipping through her own book, *The Machine-Gunneress in a State of Grace* (1977), out of print for decades. She completed it while pregnant with Velour—during Hans's final days, named for his sculpture—and she hasn't looked at it in ages. Its pages, thin and cracking, smell like a stranger. She touches Lou's skin, soft beside her. He's got his glasses on. His computer is open on his lap. A video.

CONTENT WARNING

**The following video
contains material
that may be harmful
or traumatizing
to some audiences.**

Lou clicks OKAY.
Music plays.

Lou turns the volume up. Slow music and pictures of his girlfriend's art.

-Who is Eda Singer? asks Vivienne, book resting on her lap.

-I don't know. The video was uploaded last night, though.

-Why that warning? asks Vivienne.

-They do that when they think the content will upset you, says Lou, who enjoys explaining the internet to Vivienne. It's like telling tales to a child.

-Who's they?

-I don't know.

-How do they know?

-I guess they don't.

-I want to read you some old poems.

Since those first viral tweets, Lou's been paranoid, as though whatever's coming for Vivienne might also take him. Lou is both fascinated and bored by Vivienne and her work, and he doesn't want to hear her poetry, nor does he want to look at her old sculptures—not really—which are now materializing and fading before his eyes.

The sun won't be up for hours. From the field near the house, Lou hears a cry and the cry fuses with video music. Poetry freaks him out, a freakiness underscored by the fact that the sculpture Vivienne named her book after, *The Machine-Gunneress in a State of Grace*, is being stored in their basement. Thinking of the figure, its past and frozen future, Lou shudders.

Certain corners of Velour's home are worse than the coils of compacted trash Lou rides beside daily—the rot of food and diapers, clothes and photos and biohazards—the broken meth labs. He peers over the edge of Vivienne's book, reads a few words—*between the ball and its pearly socket*—then turns back to the video, scrolling through the comments.

@syncity900? 3 hours ago

y tha fuk does this vid have 8,003 views?

Still staring at the pages of the book she wrote so long ago, Vivienne muses. Lou listens.

-There was a sitting room. A scab-colored chateau. Kind of baroque. Maudlin. I always felt *stoned*. I had the sense, back then, that I had to leave.

-Leave?

-*That* world.

Lou strokes her arm. He feels peaceful when his girlfriend waxes about the old days, the rooms she moved through—for they are now gone—over, moot. She reminds him, in these moments, of a girl he knew in high school, an odd person whom he'd recently heard, through a former classmate he ran into at the grocery store, had died during childbirth. The news delivered an apocalyptic shiver—like anything could happen, like the past was zooming full-force into the future, everything loose. That's how he feels about poetry. It unbolts things, sends them flying.

-Why'd you leave that world? Lou asks, pausing the video on an old picture of Vivienne and Velour.

@stalled6 3 hours ago
Note the black dress @ 4:00. The second time I saw
Vivienne, she was wearing that, I'm certain. I eyed her
from across the long room of an event put on by Henri
Michaux, then clumsily stumbled over. I overheard her
saying to a friend that she would stop making art, that
she had begun to feel sick at the very thought. All bodies
in the room blended together—a mass of dark wet tulle.
Truth, she said, was on the side of death.

@emmawuttt 3 hours ago
Simone Weil said that!
Not Vivienne Volker!

@obitchuary 3 hours ago
TY for sharing stories abt her she seems like an interesting
woman boneheads see fit to call her
a fascist, pervert, murderer
o well
the world

[this comment has been removed]

@fornicationstation 3 hours ago
kno that u r merely romanticizingg a woman
whose work portrays violence against u
heads and breasts on platters, etc.

@obitchuary 3 hours
John the Baptist
Saint Agatha

@fornicationstation 3 hours ago
still

131

Vivienne shrugs.

-Death, sex, war. Inescapable.

Vivienne often says things that make little actual sense. Instead, her words hit Lou a few notches below or above other conversations. In these moments, he listens. Sometimes, Vivienne is his child. Other times, his mother or grandmother. Right now, she's something foreign—neither, none. She bears no relation.

-I used to dream, she continues, that I was getting wheeled fast through a bright room.

-A hospital?

-Something like that. Unconscious.

-Dark.

-And shoved into a machine, almost dead. But not yet.

@fornicationstation 3 hours ago
why shld they reissue an almost dead headcase
instead of looking to those who r alive, unseen?
vivienne, hans, and wilma these ppl had their time
now they should listen
BYEBYEBYE

@obitchuary 2 hours ago
who should they listen to? u?

@fornicationstation 2 hours ago
all hoove been burned by art
lewk at the red velvet
embryo attached to the dress with Velcro
around 6 min
anti-abortion propaganda

@obitchuary 2 hours ago
nuh uh
fashion!

@anonanna 2 hours ago
IM HERE BC OF THE LORD
IN THE BEGINNING
GOD CREATED US
AND THE ANGELS
BORE HVNLY WITNESS
CAN U EVEN WRAP YR HEAD AROUND
BEARING WITNESS TO THE FIRST SPARKS
OF HIS WORK WHICH IS THE WORLD?

@anonanna 2 hours ago
wxmen are evil!!

@anonanna 2 hours ago
has she repented?
before the fall
we wore nothing @ all

@bridgentunnelz 2 hours ago
Volker and Bellmer
high level trolls
deeply undone
fckn insufferable

@obitchuary 2 hours ago
twas announced that Volker's work
won't appear in Forgotten Women Surrealist's
show at the NAT

@lanced80 2 hours ago
i partied w Velour ?

@stalled6 2 hours ago
VIVIENNE VOLKER'S WORK HAS BEEN REDACTED
FOR ITS POTENTIALLY HARMFUL NATURE ???
that detachable embryo is genius
doubles as a purse
i'd call it pro-choice

@stalled6 2 hours ago
a few distant encounters
with Vivienne left me
ENRAPTURED!!

-Are there angels in that book you wrote? Lou asks.

-A few.

-What's happening now?

-I'm at the circus. Walking around a stadium on Hans's drawing arm. Then my head rolls along the floor. I have no eyes. Only a mouth. With the mouth, I'm calling out to someone.

-Who?

-Maybe *you*. Vivienne smiles mischievously.

-I have to go to work soon.

@obitchuary 2 hours ago
u there?

@stalled6 2 hours ago
here

@obituary 2 hours ago
this will sound odd
but . . .

@poemposte 2 hours ago
my shoes were hooves

@obitchuary 2 hours ago
i see comments::::YOURS
in black and white dreaming
SCREENS all fckn night

@stalled6 2 hours ago
Darling Obit, what a compliment!
i myself don't dream of screens
perhaps because i'm an old man . . .
an OM ?

@poemposte 2 hours ago
i read the above as i roam
the stadium looking for you

@anonb8 2 hours ago
pseudo-mulier!!

-What happened to Wilma? Lou asks.

-I've told you about that.

-Vaguely.

-She was going to jump. Then, she finally did. I wasn't there.

-Where were you?

-Working. I told her the story of a ribbon that is a road, a story I told myself sometimes. Still do. Not sure where I first heard it. It's possible I made it up. The road is beautiful, glimmering. It's soft and shiny and it unfurls. On it, you become a soul, small and light enough to walk along its gracefulness. Uncomplicated, without parts. It takes you somewhere. To a place without tears, pain, terror. This road, of course, is a fantasy. A dream image. A screen. Life is suffering, as you know.

-Do you ever dream of screens? Lou asks, pointing to his.

-Dreams *are* screens.

-I don't know what that means.

-Screens, like dreams, are a form of mediation and expurgation without which we'd all kill ourselves. Wilma did not know how to edit out the world. She saw all of it. Then, departed.

@sigourneydreamweaver 1 hour ago
i was tken anothr whorl
where sex iz free

@775sunshine 1 hour ago
SEX AINT EVER FREE
BOUND DOLLS, PEARLESCENT DERANGED EYES,
A HOUSEFUL OF PAPER, BLOOD, EYES—
THESE PEOPLE WERE DIRT POOR IN EVERY WAY
(LIVING IN HOTELS, STEALING FROM GROCERY
STORES AND LIBRARIES . . .)

@8biblicallyacute 1 hour ago
Agree. There is a sense of profound sacrifice.
But perhaps in the next world, the one to which
@sigourneydreamweaver
alludes, sex is free and so are we . . . .
The lord is my shepherd I shall not . . . .

@signourneydreamweaver 1 hour ago
want!!

@bridgentunnelz 1 hour ago
They are what we deserve.
IF YR IN HELL
U WANT TO BE THERE
willingly took that trip
on a ship

@obitchuary 1 hour ago
in your heart u know she's right

@177nullify 1 hour ago
Another shooting today.
Pray for these beings in search of meaning.
Pray for want of attention and celebrity
To be replaced by attention of generosity.

@8biblicallyacute 1 hour ago
Amen.

@sigourneydreamweaver 1 hour ago
boom

@stalled6 1 hour ago
We might say Vivienne's work predicted this.

@bananasfoster 1 hour ago
"I THINK ART IS THE ABSENCE OF FEAR" -Erykah Badu

[this comment has been removed]

@poemposte 1 hour ago
Into the sequined river
and whatever else is out there

@sally4660128 1 hour ago
WHO ELSE IS OUT THERE??? human beings!
regardless of gender, we are in this together,
together
I mean look! one blue sky which we need to consider in
how we interact with each other
HUGS
inside the terrible crystal
we are all incubating inside of
and under

-In his final days, I read him Abelard and Heloise. Their letters.

-I don't know who those people are, Lou says.

-They were a very famous couple from the Middle Ages. He got castrated.

-Why?

-She was a holy woman, his student.

-You're a holy woman, Lou says, kissing her.

-This is a poem about a horse. I wrote it a lifetime ago. I'll read it to you.

-We found a horse's head in a dumpster once. Some asshole just tossed it.

-What did you do? Vivienne asks, putting her book down.

-First, I backed up. I thought it might explode.

-Darling, why would it explode?

-The gases keep building up, even after death. Human bodies explode sometimes, too. Methane. *Boom.*

-Obscene. Poor thing. Where was the body?

-We never found it. Maybe it exploded. The head, we dealt with. I remember the mane. It was still pretty, soft. That surprised me.

Vivienne stokes Lou's hair.

-I wonder who found the decapitated body. Bodies can do things after death, Vivienne says.

-True. Flies were swarming its head. We put it in a special bag, the ones we use for animal remains, then took it to the landfill.

-You're quite brilliant at what you do.

-That day sucked.

@thotleader11 1 hour ago
I'm here because I have fallen in love with a man many
years older and have heard that Vivienne was like 40 years
younger than Hans, tho don't think age gap is part of the
discourse around this scandal. been sobbing all nite
Not usually big on this platform,
can feel self being watched
will likely delete this l8r. Been looking
at Bellmer's sculptures.
Vivienne's too. They're fine, whatever.
I think I just need to type
all this out for myself and my searches have led
me to the bottom of Surrealism
SRY 4 MELODRAMA and have been
considering the similarities
vis a vis something a friend said
re: my story and Viv's. I DO NOT EXPECT
any of you angels
to respond to this but i will leave my notifications
nonetheless ON <3
BELIEVE ME I KNOW THERE IS NO FILLING THE VOID
BUT THIS MAN IS DESTROYING AND COMPLETING
MY HOLE LIFE Xo, TL

@nbbvdealing 45 minutes ago
GO KILL YOURSELF @thotleader11

@ghostofhandsbellmer 45 minutes ago
hi @thotleader11—from what I know about this platform
they remove suicide encouragements quickly
likely that user will be banned too
anyway what is the nature

141

of your relationship with this man?
i hope you are seeking help on another plane
outside the comments section i mean ?

@obitchuary 40 minutes ago
what's the age gap, babe?

@stalled6 40 minutes ago
Viv's work tends to attract those in the heights of despair,
such as Thot Leader here.

@obitchuary 34 minutes ago
u okay @thotleader11 ??

@nbbvdealing 32 minutes ago
chill she prolly just typing

@ghostofhandsbellmer 32 minutes ago
perhaps go away @nbbvdealings

@nbbvdealings 31 minutes ago
YOU @$$h0l3!!!

@thotleader11 28 minutes ago
"KILL YOURSELF!" helped me so much!
like a splash of cold water on my neck. i'm calmer now.
but still contemplating (duh) jumping out window.
the man is 38 years my senior, the exact # of years
Hans had on Vivienne.
weird, huh? anyway, we are married but not to each other ha

@ghostofhandsbellmer 25 minutes ago
Hans was post-stroke when Wilma
jumped from that window,
the window, all windows: glass metaphors
for the nature of relations
between males and females. For Wilma,
windows and windowpanes were very important.
The crosses
they make.

@obitchuary 22 minutes ago
Does he love u?

@thotleader11 20 minutes ago
says so all the time
he knew Vivienne back in the day and
when her name went viral,
he got kinda obsessed
she was the kind of woman, he sd,
that ppl get obsessed about
so i came here to check it outttttttt

@ghostofhandsbellmer 19 minutes ago
hans was old and cancerous couldn't really take care of W,
not in the way she needed. She was mad, I say MAD as a
compliment. i think Lacan treated her. or some heavy hitter
like that. and she jumped shortly after hans ended their
relationship. perhaps in part because, of course, he had met
VV. Who knows, though. VV was much much younger than
Wilma and i guess he loved her BUT his sculptures suggest he
had something of a love-hate relationship with . . . .everything

@obitchuary 18 minutes ago
unholy trinity ?

@thotleader11 18 minute ago
WINDOW INTO WHAT WORLD THO

@obitchuary 16 minutes ago
& what finally broke the dam? is that the right phrase?
what made you, in other words,
end up in THIS trash heap w/ us?

@nbbvdealings 15 minutes ago
wit tha stans and trolls
sorting thru vivienne's remains

@thotleader11 13 minutes ago
HAHA @nbbvdealings SEE ABOVE !!
vivienne was a distant object which Old Man,
(OM) the universal vibration,
was fixated upon. i began to enter one of those swirly,
thousand-eyed dreams
fantasizing about my lifes end
instead, i took to the comments section.

@ghostofhandsbellmer 12 minutes ago
beautifully stated, thot !
sounds like you got trapped
in the space between things and words
which only continues to widen

@thotleader11 10 minutes ago
I dunno know what that means but there is a big rift
between us
like the rift between things and words, sure? he's
obsessed with artists (like VV)
whereas i find normal people far more interesting
OM has all three of her books and he freaked when i
asked if they were maybe out of print cause they were bad

@obitchuary 8 minute ago
you have more integrity in your pinky toe than he does in
his whole BEING, @thotleader11
if possible, try to take a pic of Viv's books
i know a lot of us here are curious
hard to find images

@nbbvdealings 7 minutes ago
how can you possibly know that re integrity, @obtichuary ?!
we don't know who Thot really is
why tell her to enter OM's home
and take pics?!!!

@thotleader11 6 minutes ago
yr right @nbbvdealings
& thnx again for the "GO KILL YOURSELF"
made me feel alive inside
sent you a private msg

-People are really interested in you.

Vivienne shrugs. Lou can't get the phrase *Vivienne's Remains* out of his head. He's never seen any human remains at work, though he's handled prosthetic limbs before.

-You were beautiful, Lou says, pointing to the video. Vivienne raises an eyebrow.

-*Are* beautiful. People are saying sweet things. And insane things. Not all bad, though.

-I don't know if I achieved it in this book.

-Achieved what?

-A vision of freedom in which the terror of gravity is momentarily escaped as suffering and ecstasy enter into the body.

-Oh *that*? I bet you achieved that, Lou says. His face is lit violet and blue in the pre-dawn room as he reads comments which look blurry to Vivienne. He raises his eyebrows and she laughs, throwing her head back. They sit in silence, her book splayed open on her legs. There's something mad about Vivienne's laugh. Must be genetic, Lou thinks, as Velour does it, too—the two women like drugged and deluded birds. Sometimes, she throws her head back so fast Lou thinks she'll get whiplash. He's tried to do the same backwards motion with his own head, but it just doesn't move like that. His own mother's laugh is quiet and rare. There's a fade-out quality to his mother—faint, fuzzy. Vivienne and Velour, on the other hand, are hard and distinct. They're made from some difficult-to-dis-pose-of heavy metal that conducts electricity. Lou thinks of the non-fer-rous metals like lead, gold, and tin, which can be recycled much more easily than ferrous ones like cast iron or steel. *The Machine-Gunneress in a State of Grace* is made of metal and wood.

-What are you thinking about? Vivienne asks.

-Nothing. That doll in the basement.

-I'd love to see it, she says, blinking, thin and persistent as a cursor, into the black center of the room.

-But you hate that thing.

-I don't. I just choose not to interact, Vivienne says, staring into the distance as she does—looking at something invisible. Lou stares at the same spot, and they get quiet.

-Why do you think Velour keeps it locked up in the basement? he asks.

-She hopes it's accruing value. Karmic, psychic, financial, I guess.

-*Karmic* value, Lou repeats, sounds like her.

-Can you bring it up here before you leave for work? Vivienne whispers. She seems to be gone, as though whatever she's staring at has kidnapped her.

-Are you okay?

-Can you get the doll?

-I'd rather not. Lou wonders if this is a test. He senses, at times, that the women are testing him. Their constant obscure references to bizarre figures, the errands they send him on. Even Vesta tests him, with her suspicious looks and bitchy asides. He envisions himself throwing the sculpture in the truck and watching as it gets crushed into a cube with the town's garbage. He's seen used sex dolls in there before, and when he pictures Bellmer's sculpture alongside the heaps they pick up each day, a warmth permeates his body. Remnants and remains riding through town in a truck filled with art.

After he changes into his work jumpsuit, he walks quietly down the hallway and peeks into Vesta's room, as he does every morning on his way down. It's a compulsion at this point, fearing that if he does not confirm her existence, she'll disappear. There's an effervescent unrealness about the girl, fortified by the way the dog follows her everywhere. She's sleeping, arm around the mutt. Franz looks up, tilts his head. Lou retreats, then descends down the spiral stairs quietly, at medium speed. When he sees Velour on the couch, robe and mouth open, legs sprawled and quietly snoring, his heart pounds. He stands over her, reaching his arm out, then backs away and walks toward the basement door, like in a dream. He opens it to a rush of cold air and flips on the light. Velour stirs. He walks down the old wooden stairs.

In the damp basement, Lou has to crouch so he doesn't hit his head. Above him, cobwebs. There are three rooms but no doors, an old television, an oil tank, toys, a wooden door to the outside, and the doll. The doll is not a doll. Not really. It's right here: in a clear and locked box, emitting a mauve light, an assemblage of air and ball joints. He steps closer, surprised that he can hear Velour's loud breathing above him and above that, music, and Vesta's teeth grinding. He hears rustling in the field, the squawk of a creature sweeping through cold grass, and the first chirping birds. He won't be able to put the entire see-through rectangular box on his back and take it up to Viv. Still, he attempts to lift the alien thing and its clunky case as though he's being directed. He coughs, winces. He tries again, lifting it higher off the ground this time. How much time has passed?

-What are you *doing*? Velour asks.

Lou sets the doll's case down and sits down on the floor beneath Velour as she unlocks the plexiglass door and touches the doll clinically, as though checking its vitals. From below, Velour and the doll are one contraption: pinkish, thin, lit from within. Lou's arm reaches up as though it's remote-controlled—like it's not his arm at all—in one long pawing gesture toward Velour's robe. Unsure why he's on the floor, he jolts when his hand makes contact. Lou senses they're being held between ball and socket, suspended in muscle jelly, not quite alone.

Velour's dirty white robe falls to the floor and he lies down on the velvety, animalesque mass. His heart pounds. She stands naked in front of the doll. Lou touches a spot of dried blood mixed with mud on her thigh. The clear case hangs open like a mouth. *The Machine-Gunneress* frames her, smooth flippers beneath an eyeless head and clown breast. Velour, a tentacular woman-girl-machine, convulses. Her head jolts back as though glitching before she falls toward him, the thick basement air retarding her dive. Up close, her eyes are shut and her face contorts into a grimace. Lou's own face repeats the expression and their bodies entwine on cold concrete.

She's amorphous . . . something like a horse, her mouth reaching for Lou's back, coffin bone knifing the softer parts of his spine. Lou shoves himself into a hole and Velour buckles, moans. Warmth. Her sounds travel into him and get stuck, turning. When he opens his eyes, all's blurry, like he's trying to see through a layer of marrow. He blinks and when the creature finally comes into focus, her mouth is a beak. There's a gust of wind. Another shift—electrically arcing into hot plasma, blood spreading around him. Their bodies go slack simultaneously and when she relaxes back into herself, Lou's struck by the terrible and alluring sensation that he'll have to live inside this residue forever, the way the letters of his own name are nested in the letters of hers, a fact he hadn't thought of until just now. Silence.

-What are you looking at? asks Velour.

His body is zapped, like he's been hanging off the back of the truck. He zips his jumpsuit up and runs a finger over his embroidered nametag, to verify: here. Velour closes the case and locks the doll back up.

-I have to go to work, Lou says, reaching up.

She helps him to his feet.

Upstairs, Vivienne smiles into the bluing blackness.

VELOUR

December 18

Morning

Outside the kitchen window: cool, edgeless white. At the table wearing a clean, oversized white sweater and silk pants. Velour stares out the window into the space where the yard, field, trees, and LOST DOG sign would be. All images have dissolved in total and glittering winter. She drops her half-smoked cigarette into her mug of cold coffee. Her eyes are two pearls, slippery and vacant. She's still bleeding, but the blood is lighter, thinner, running faster now.

Velour's been enveloped in a hungover sensation ever since she emerged, burning, from the basement yesterday morning. Avoiding both her mother and Lou has been easy. The house is like that sometimes—bending and contorting in order to hide whomever requires it. The freezing sun cancels that thought. All thought. No thinking about art. No Velour. No Vivienne. No Vesta. No Lou. Especially no Lou. The light fills and empties Velour's head, then the kitchen, and finally takes the house.

When she hears her daughter singing, she jumps. The yard and all the contents of the field and her head—images upon images—reconstituting.

-Less than a week! Vesta screams.

-Huh?

-Christmas! *Duh.*

The girl and the dog are in the blurry white yard now, and Velour rests her chin on the kitchen table, watching them blot out as they frolic. She looks at her screen and reads the newest comments:

@obitchuary 1 hour ago
i heard Gallery X will show
Vivienne's work

@stalled6 1 hour ago
when?

@obitchuary 1 hour ago
in 2 days
thats the rumor

@anonb8 30 minutes ago
anyone here gonna go?

@poemposte 28 minutes ago
i'll be there

@obitchuary 28 minutes ago
curious to see what she's like
IRL

@stalled6 27 minutes ago
think she'll be there?

@poemposte 26 minutes ago
yes

@anonb8 25 minutes ago
REVENGE ON CULTURE

@thotleader11 24 minutes ago
i bet she'll be present
emerge from the rubble

@nbvdealings 24 minutes ago
Hey @thotleader11
hope to see you

@edasinger 22 minutes ago
the event has not yet been confirmed

@anonb8 20 minutes ago
VV deserves to get pummeled
THUD

@poemposte 20 minutes ago
sculpture at minute 27
emitting bright light
from source

[this comment has been removed]

LARS

December 19

Morning

From the Jersey side of the tunnel, Lars tilts his sunglasses down and glances back at the sky above Manhattan. His stomach is growling and his car tells him he's merely two hours and eleven minutes from his destination: the home of Vivienne Volker in the woods of Pennsylvania. He finds this fact startling, as Pennsylvania seems so bizarre, foreign. When he hears the word, he pictures miles and miles of georgic scenes like *Christina's World* and some drowsy cows. He knows plenty of folks who have moved upstate and some who own getaways in places like Nantucket or Maine.

But *Pennsylvania?*

Lars started the morning with an early spin class. He's starving but doesn't like to eat until eleven, at which point: hard-boiled egg. (He's got a black coffee in the Yeti, which he'll permit himself to start in about fifteen minutes.) He's watched the video of Vivienne's work at least five times. He's also cued up a podcast, released yesterday in response to the controversy. All in all, he feels optimistic, pure, prepped.

Cruising through the reek of a Jersey oil refinery, he takes his first swig of coffee and plays the podcast, a show called *WAIT, WHAT?*, where Brad and Charlie, two bicoastal elites, talk about culture. As they gab about holiday plans and grooming habits, Lars imagines a pastoral meeting between himself and Vivienne wherein they sit for tea inside a mansion surrounded by rolling hills, an aged Great Dane snoozing at their feet, and Velour offering refills. In his detailed visualization, which he already played in his head once while pumping the pedals on the stationary bike, Vivienne agrees to do the show right away and he can get back in his car and return to New York. When he tells her he wants to ride the momentum of the internet debacle and do a livestreamed walk-through as soon as *tomorrow*, she accepts right away. He'll visualize a few more times. He *needs* to manifest this show. His team has already started dropping hints to the public.

Lars registers snippets of audio—

Oh the Surrealists love weird animals, right?

That's absolutely a thing

'Tis the season

Do you think this woman gives a shit—like, what do you think her story is?

There's not much, honestly, not much

Who is this gossipy ex?

Morphine, opium

Picasso loved that shit

It's supposed to be fucked with

Lost limbs

Soldiers, war

Before drones

Sure, sure

A superior reality

As far as I can tell, they're just doll clothes? I'm dense, but

I legitimately want this woman to have a merry Christmas

Fuck yeah

She was around

But this was like, before we were born
Were you in Paris?
No this guy's work is in-fucking-sane
I'm into it
Am I missing something
Would I want it in my house? Well, no
So we can just stop larping as cultured people
This is from the 1930s, kind of the heyday
Ain't no stocking stuffer
That used to be my favorite brunch spot
So Vivienne came along later
Nudged Wilma out that window
Allegedly! Allegedly
Maybe not
Can you imagine
I'd like to meet her
Sure, have dinner
Do you think she's listening
What restaurant would you take her to
One with bars around the windows

The smugly jovial voices of the hosts, coupled with hunger, drive Lars to feelings of violence, fear, and loneliness. He thinks of his heroes—Martin Margiela, Marguerite Porete, Saint Anthony and the desert fathers, and now—Vivienne Volker. He reaches into his Rick Owens quilted leather crossbody bag for his hard-boiled egg and begins to sweat. It's not there. *Fuck you, motherfuckers,* he yells at Brad and Charlie. He forgot to pack sustenance. OK. No problem. Saint Anthony didn't eat for *days.* Lars forgets how long the saint went without food but whatever, he'll stop at a gas station on the way and get some bullshit. Maybe sugar. He deserves it—hasn't eaten anything since yesterday afternoon. He turns off the podcast and rolls down the windows, recalling some lines from Marguerite Porete's spiritual guidebook from the fourteenth century:

The Unencumbered Soul, says Love, is balanced by means of a yoke with two equal weights, that is, one on the right and other on the left. With these two weights the Soul is strong against her enemies, like a castle on a hill . . .

Soul is strong against her enemies, like a castle on a hill, like a castle on a hill, like a castle on a hill, he repeats.

~

He passes PENNSYLVANIA WELCOMES YOU sometime after his rage subsides. Apparently, he's twenty-five minutes from Vivienne Volker's home. He needs to eat something before he speaks to her. Needs to be strong. Like a castle on a hill. The map shows nothing but green fields all around his moving car, but the green fields are yellowing-gray, filled with melting snow, grimy under the white sky. Lars huffs in the driver's seat, wishing he could crawl out of his skin and rest in one of Vivienne's doll garments like a stuffed animal behind crinoline, delicate and protected.

He catches his reflection in the mirror and smooths his eyebrows, pleasantly surprised. He looks less ugly than he feels. On the side of the road, a bearded guy and a woman in a prairie dress stand beside a table with a SHOO-FLY PIE sign. Trembling a little, Lars pulls over. The man is wearing a wide-brimmed hat. The woman wears what looks to Lars like a bonnet, but maybe she's pinned a handkerchief to her head.

-You guys look awesome!

-Thank you, the man says in an accent Lars doesn't recognize.

-Can I get a slice to go, with a fork?

-We're selling whole pies. No forks.

-What are the ingredients?

-Butter, molasses, eggs.

-Organic, right?

-Organic, yes.

-You know what? Fuck it. Whole pie! Whole pie! Sell anything else?

-Raw milk, the man says, pointing to a blue cooler.

-That's legal here? They'll arrest you in New York.

-Legal, yes, the woman says, nodding.

-What are your thoughts on pasteurization?

They scowl.

-Oh it's like *that*, Lars says.

She laughs.

-I've heard raw milk is good for the microbiome, says Lars, patting his stomach.

-Yes.

-Cash okay?

-We take only cash.

Sitting in the car, he digs into the gooey brown pie with his fingers. He'll only eat a few bites, just enough to stave off chatty delirium or unbridled rage. As it slides down his throat, he moans and looks into the distance, registering the place for the first time: a field, low mountains, a strip mall with lit-up signs he can't read, and dirty patches of white repeating over green. Vivienne's work appears in front of him like a screen. Strips of fabric and plastic alchemized into a costume, the faraway hills wearing one of her hats, and her 1970s mouth hanging over the dotted scenery. He licks his fingers.

Near the peak of carbohydrate ecstasy, Lars has an inkling that everything will be alright—all worries delinked from their originary springs. He can sense something ineffable at his edges—his *soul*, he hopes, getting altered: ripped and hemmed. He frowns at the pie, which he's eaten a third of, then leans back and sucks the molasses from his fingers, closing his eyes. He envisions Velour Bellmer in one of her party poses as his brain, heart, joints, and liver flood with goo and butter. The fog disbands over the road and he opens the glass bottle of raw milk. Chugs the thick, sweet liquid as bells chime over the halcyon expanse: it's noon.

He starts the car and drives toward Vivienne.

~

One minute from her home, he sees a few blurry figures in the distance situated in a field lined with tall trees. In the yard, a woman in a long black coat hunches over a small girl who appears to be a miniature version of the older woman. They are wearing the same style jacket, black with mutton sleeves. Lars squints. The girl is holding something which the woman is interested in. As he gets closer, Lars can see that the girl is distressed. Two other figures bookend them: a man in a blue jumpsuit and a woman in white.

He parks on the road, the house about twenty yards in the dappled distance. The little girl is weeping. A tall, muscular, savage-looking dog patrols the perimeter. Lars pauses, flinching as he pictures himself getting mauled as the family looks on. A woman (Velour?) crouches down and embraces the girl, trying to grab whatever object she's cradling. A fail. The woman walks away, throws her arms up in the air.

The man in blue puts his hands on his hips while Vivienne looks up at the sky.

Lars takes one last gulp of raw milk before stepping onto the grass.

As he gets closer, everything's amplified in stereophonic horror: the girl's cries are louder and the woman in white, who he can see now is certainly Velour, looks panicked. No one notices him. Terrified of the dog, he takes a few more steps into the weird arena, eyes wide, Margiela boots sinking into damp ground. Inhaling the crisp fresh air, smelling wet wheat and mist and a wood fire and something sweet, he doesn't even care about the mud on his soles. The dog clocks Lars first, and charges.

-Fuck! Lars yells, shielding his crotch.

-Franz, *off! Off!* yells the guy in the jumpsuit.

Velour runs over, grabbing the dog's collar and pulling him away from Lars, her hand firm, pushing her fingers hard into his neck. Franz's body goes slack and he turns, galumphing over to the girl.

-He doesn't usually bite, but brute force works best, Velour says, smiling. She introduces herself and Lars extends the back of his hand, having seen his girlfriend do that. Velour stares. Lars has the sudden urge to embrace Vivienne, who hasn't yet acknowledged him. He resists. All eyes return, again, to whatever the little girl, whose back is to Lars, is holding. Finally, the dog grabs it. The girl screams and, chasing after him, falls in the mud. She gets up. Franz runs to Lars and drops the thing at his feet, now wet with drool. Lars huddles down, inspecting the specimen, feeling outdoorsy and capable for a second.

-Oh my *god*, Lars says, it's a *foot*.

The little girl, face covered in mud, looks up at Lars through tears.

-That's Pepper's, she says, pointing to the leg.

Velour points to the LOST DOG sign tacked to a tree in the corner of the yard.

-It's the neighbor's chihuahua. *Was* the neighbor's chihuahua.

It's a small, brown, mangled extremity: fur, bone, muscle, mud. Lou winces.

-I'm guessing a hawk got her, Lou tells Lars. Lars nods solemnly, though he's never heard of a hawk doing such a thing. He plays the dramatic taloned swoop in slow motion in his head, vivifying.

-That *sucks*, Lars says.

-Do you think it was peaceful? Vesta asks.

-Are you asking *me*? Lars says, looking around.

-Thank you for coming, Vivienne interrupts, it's lovely to meet you.

He cannot believe she's over eighty. Wants to ask about her skincare regimen.

-It's really my pleasure. I appreciate you taking the time. I know you're busy.

-Not really. That's Vesta, my granddaughter. And that's my love, Lou. And you've met Velour, Vivienne says.

-Imagine getting digested by a hawk, Lou says, shaking his head.

-I guess I *have* to call Lisa. Fuck! Velour interrupts.

-Pepper was Lisa's dog, Lou tells Lars.

-She already hates me. Maybe I'll call Mac instead, Velour says, spinning around.

-That'll set her off more, Lou says.

-She doesn't *hate* you, Vesta reassures.

Lars feels stoned. New roads, pie, milk, dog foot.

Velour stomps away, back towards the house. She seems to be clutching her phone in one hand and the mangled appendage in the other, but Lars doesn't see why she'd still be holding the thing. Has he begun to hallucinate? Certain kinds of bacteria can do that, he recalls.

-So you're going to show Viv's work? asks Lou.

-That's my hope. *Great* jumpsuit, says Lars.

-It's my uniform, Lou says.

When Velour returns, Lars notes her outfit: an oversized white sweater, angora maybe, and green rain boots.

-Lisa's on her way. Should we *show her* the leg?

-Obviously, Lou says.

Vivienne is comforting Vesta. The two whisper back and forth. Lars can't make out what they're saying.

-Maybe seeing the leg will bring closure, Lars offers.

-Closure, Velour repeats.

-The creature is no longer lost, Vivienne says.

Lars scans the yard, trying to figure out where the leg is now. He stares at Vivienne, a skinny, chic, birdlike woman looking up at the sky. He runs through the speech in his head—his pitch. Vesta gets up and brushes off her coat, then walks over to Lars and touches his bag.

-I like your purse, the girl says.

-Thanks. It's more of a *crossbody bag*. He feels instant kinship with the moody girl, her swings similar to his hunger-induced manias. Now, he's quelled from thick molasses, milk, and the cool comfort of someone else's drama. He looks around, wondering what these people eat, then tries to guess how many calories are in an entire shoofly pie. Numbers flash: 3,000, 3,800, 4,000.

Vesta giggles. She looks like she's been torn from a coffee table book his mother had on Edwardian and Victorian era fashion. The two are sizing each other up when a big black SUV pulls over, a broad man with a full head of gray hair in the driver's seat and a blonde woman riding shotgun. Lars backs up, instinctively pinching the skin around his stomach. He's a little bloated. The vascular, tan blonde thrusts herself out of the car and makes a beeline for Velour. Lars thinks the she might hit her.

-Where is she? Where's Pepper?

-Mrs. Wallace, yells Vesta, suddenly poised, calm, diplomatic, we only have her leg. Franz found it in the field.

-A hawk took her, Lou says.

-Red-tailed, Vivienne says.

-Dear God. That's *Pepper's leg*? Oh god, her little nails. Lisa whines. Velour nods, offering the remains.

-Drop it in here, Lou says, holding open a plastic bag.

Lisa sticks her tongue out. The man steps out of the car.

A prehistoric bird with a long neck circles above their heads.

-Vulture, Lou tells Lars, pointing.

-You people are *fucked*, Lisa says. She grabs the Ziplock bag which holds Pepper's leg, then mean-mugs Lars. Should he introduce himself? No, likely not.

-Lisa, *please*, the broad man says.

-Mac! Whose side are you on? Lisa is waving the bag furiously, foot bouncing around inside. Her long nails are painted silver, green, and red and they shimmer under the hard sky. All the light bounces off the snowy ground, superluminous. Lars squints, still feeling mildly drugged.

-That's an old world vulture, Lou tells Vivienne, pointing at the bird.

-What's that? she asks.

-Mrs. Wallace, Vesta pleads, tell Mackenzie I'm sorry. The girl begins crying again and Lars squats down.

-It's totally *not* your fault, he says. Vesta strokes the black leather strap of Lars's bag.

-That man is right, honey, says Lisa, I'm just not *myself* lately. You know I'm usually the *fun* Mom! You *know* it. Pepper was my girl. My twin. The holidays. I don't know. I'm sorry. Wait! I'm *not* sorry. No! You know what? No. I have to stop apologizing for *expressing* myself. I keep *seeing* her. Running around, all sassy, and then *BAM*! Kidnapped. Gone! Like what's his name. Ganymede!

Lars watches the raw pink muscle flap inside the bag. Lisa gags a little, then gets suddenly still.

-What? Lisa asks Lars.

-I'm sorry. Sorry for your loss, Lars says, bowing his head.

-Babe, Mac interjects, let's get back home. We'll bury . . . that.

-Pepper was a good girl, Velour tells Lisa, waving goodbye.

Mac leads Lisa back into the front seat, placing the bag on her lap.

-Merry Christmas, Mac says.

$\sim$

To Lars Arden, the Volker-Bellmer residence is a hidden continent to which he's been suddenly admitted—proof, somehow, that there are many worlds within and around his. Yes, the house definitely has a *soul*. As he crosses the threshold, he wonders if the dog's leg, which was flying around the yard haphazardly, may have left some noxious residuum on him. He walks toward the toilet awestruck, confounded by the size and shape of this place, which doesn't match its simple exterior. Mazelike and vertiginous, filled with crevices and sudden shifts in temperament. The living room is dark with black and brown wallpaper, its ceiling painted blue and white to look like the sky. At the center, a debutante-style chandelier with glass strands. The bathroom is covered in turquoise wallpaper with flowers, leaves, and peacocks. After he pisses, he smooths his brows, checks his teeth, examines the dark circles under his eyes, and makes faces. The mirror has beveled edges. Under it, an old clock which is no longer ticking and a brass box. When he steps back out into the living room, he feels he's being watched.

Maybe he's just coming down off the shoofly, or else he's acquired some fast-acting brain-eating bacteria from the raw milk. Why—*why!*—did he choose to take a culinary risk *today* of all days? By the time Lars staggers back into the kitchen, he's sure it's the house, not the raw dairy, that's fucking with him. There are two, maybe three, sets of stairs. The floor is solid wood and makes raspy, throaty noises when stepped on. The wallpaper, which he now realizes is patterned with eyes, is absurdist surveillance.

When he returns to the kitchen, Vivienne speaks in trance-inducing whispers, hospitable: *have a seat, make yourself comfortable. Do you need anything? Velour, honey, get him some coffee.* He sits down and inhales, trying to steady himself. The little girl is eyeing him. From across the shiny white table, he waves at her dumbly.

-Great house. Old, right?

-Two-hundred years, Velour says.

-Shit, is that a real Bellmer? he points to the framed drawing on the wall above the table.

-Yes, Velour confirms.

-That's where my dad died, says Vesta.

-What? He looks around at the adults. All stare.

-That chair, Vesta says, smiling.

-The one I'm in?

Velour nods, amused. A real smile.

-I'm sorry. Should I get up? Lars says.

Velour chuckles.

-Where did you grow up? she asks, leaning in.

-New York.

-Where specifically?

-Uptown.

Velour nods and lights a cigarette. Vivienne is smoking a clove and staring out into the misty yard. Vesta is on the floor now, Franz draped over her lap, slack and boneless. Lou eyes Velour from across the table.

The child wiggles out from under the dog, stands up, and heads for Lars, touching his hand.

-*Fuck!* she exclaims, wide-eyed.

-Vesta! Vivienne says.

-That's what it says on his hand! Look!

When Lars holds his knuckles up, Velour looks disappointed.

-F-U-C-K: one letter on each knuckle, Vivienne reports.

-I was young, Lars says.

They sit in silence. He's allowing the weirdly wired house and its women to wash over him. Velour and Vivienne ash simultaneously into a colorful, disconcerting receptacle.

-Trippy ashtray, Lars says, pointing.

-*A Little Night Music*, the child sing-songs.

-What?

-That's the name of the painting! Vesta says, pointing to the ashtray.

-Is it your work? Lars asks Vivienne.

-It's Dorothea Tanning! Vesta shrieks.

-Oh, right. Of course, Lars says.

Another silence. Lars looks around the kitchen, the air suddenly cold. He takes a breath and begins his pitch.

-I want to show your work because I truly believe it deserves to be seen, collected, revived. Your art *will* outlive this bullshit. I would, however, propose that we ride this media wave, in order to get the maximum amount of . . . *eyes.*

-What is it about her work that interests you? Velour inquires.

-Don't *test* him, Vivienne says.

-I've been falling asleep to a video compilation of your work, Vivienne. A totally, for lack of a better word, *psychedelic* experience—seeing so much of it in one place, one image after another. Watching that video made me *know* I had to do the show. That it *had to be me.* Your work and life seemed to be . . .uh . . .entering me, if that doesn't sound too gay.

-You're bald like Grandpa, Vesta says, leaning in.

-I shave it, he says, rubbing his head.

-He *does* look like Hans a little, doesn't he? Vivienne says, eyes glimmering. Lars detects a hint of madness or devotion—something fervent—in her. He feels his mutilated soul on display.

-Damn, thanks. Bellmer is a *towering* figure.

-Well, we all go bald in the end, Vivienne says.

-Really? Vesta asks.

-Yes, Vivienne says, nodding slowly. Lou laughs and places his hand on Viv's. Lars coughs and squints, smoke everywhere, and begins the second part of his pitch.

-Here's my *ask*. Would you, Vivienne, be willing to come to the city tomorrow?

There's a long, pained silence. Lars looks around. In this house, Lars wonders if he is ridiculous. His outfit makes so much sense downtown. But next to Lou, dressed in an actual uniform, inside a house that's been here for centuries, he feels like a fraud. He wonders how many people have died here. He looks down at the white kitchen chair, reminding himself that he's a good gallerist with a decent reputation and plenty of knowledge.

-Yes, Mr. Arden, Vivienne says.

-Really? Yes? Wow. *Yes.* Well, I'll take care of it. We'll set everything up and you can view the installation tomorrow evening. Tomorrow, it'll be just the two of us doing a chill walkthrough. And it will act as a kind of soft opening. A preview. We'll have a livestream set up so people can watch from anywhere. People are dying to see you. Rightfully so. We can have someone drive you into the city tomorrow. Once you give me the green light, I'll have my people get the sculptures from the NAT and start the install ASAP. The whole thing. Here are some photos of the gallery, and a digital sketch of what the garments will look like there, so you can get a sense for how your work will be interacting with the space.

-I don't need to see the pictures.

Lars stutters, fumbling with his phone.

-You're sure?

-Yes.

-Can I come? Vesta asks.

-I think I should go alone, darling, Vivienne says.

-Can you *believe* she compared her dog to Ganymede? Velour says, laughing.

-Who is *Ganymede*? Vesta interjects.

-*Ganymede*, Vivienne tells Vesta, was a beautiful boy who was kidnapped by Zeus. Zeus fell in love.

-Maybe the hawk loved Pepper, Lou says. Vivienne smiles and squeezes his hand. Vesta scowls.

-Pepper wasn't *kidnapped*, Lou, Vesta says.

-Ganymede, Vivienne continues, is now made of stars. Somewhere in the Aquarius constellation, if I'm not mistaken.

-I'm named after stars, Vesta tells Lars, her face brightening.

-Vesta is an asteroid, Lars says.

Velour nods and Lars gets a hit of relief: mild approval from Bellmer's daughter. Vesta smiles, batting her mother's smoke away from her face. She rests her chin on her hand and looks at Lars. Lars wonders for how long he should maintain eye contact with the girl.

-Do you think Pepper could be like . . . *living* with the birds? Up there, Vesta asks him, her head moving back and forth. The child points to the ceiling and Lars looks.

~

GALLERY X GROUP TEXT

LARS 3:44 pm
she said YES

CLORINDA 3:46 pm
YES, congrats baby

SIXTINE 3:46 pm
Congrats to us
we'll get it rolling

LARS 3:47 pm
R and S:
livestream setup
social promo
press release
TONITE OK?

RONI 3:47 pm
YES

SIXTINE 3:49 pm
LIVESTREAM/VIVIENNE ARRIVAL
beginning tomorrow when?

LARS 3:50 pm
say 6pm

CLORINDA 3:52 pm
perf
re: the publicity plan we discussed
need to finalize a signal of some sort

LARS 3:54 pm
will discuss tomorrow morn
LONG DAY

SIXTINE 3:54 pm

K

RONI 3: 54 pm

confirmed

see you soon

LARS 3: 56 pm

thanks team

mad rush

almost done

~

Today doesn't count, thinks Lars as he drives east, cloud-covered sunset flooding his rearview. He palms the rest of the pie as he drives, then finishes off the milk. *No, today doesn't count. No.* The voices of the women come back to him in crackly static. Lisa's screams, Velour's bitchy inquiries, Vivienne's apparent kindness. And especially Vesta, Vesta touching his knuckles and uttering *fuck*, her sobs and insistent eye contact. He can feel the girl watching him from the sky as he drives, a kid turned constellation. He touches his head and a dark calm washes over his body as he merges onto the highway. The preview tomorrow night should go as smoothly as possible, as Vesta and Velour watch from that melodious, Kafkaesque house. Vivienne and Lars will walk the perimeter of the gallery calmly, calmly . . . no stunts, no bullshit . . . just walking. The sun disappears behind the mountains. Soon, eyes heavy, Lars will cross over into the next state.

~

@anonb8 3 minutes ago
any word?????

@edasinger 2 minutes ago
Gallery X just announced
Preview / soft opening
TOMORROW NIGHT
DEC 20th
6pm

@obitchuary 2 minutes ago
will she be there

@nicoredhead 2 minutes ago
Does GALLERY X HAVE
ANY FUCKING DIGNITY?

@syncity900? 1 minute ago
SHE IS GOING TO
WALK AROUND THE SPACE
WHILE WE WATCH
ZOO

@poemposte 1 minute ago
im going to try to attend

@thotleader11 1 minute ago
see you there
ill be wearing a red hat

@nbvdealings 1 minute ago
Looking fwd to meeting you, Thot
i will b carrying a doll

175

@stalled6 1 minute ago
tuning in from home

@thotleader11 now
happy holidaze <3
suicide on the rise this time of year
Let's b kind!!

@maud005 now
of course Lars Arden of Gallery X
is showing this nonsense
blood on his hands

@stalled6 now
has anyone ever considered the following:
if the rumor is true, (and Vivienne DID incite Wilma's suicide
somehow) that it was, perhaps, an act of kindness?
allowing her to die with dignity

@obitchuary now
mercy?

[this comment has been removed]

@edasinger now
Yes

@poemposte now
invisible rubble
what's so great about dignity

@maud005 now
Hateful

VESTA

December 20

6:00 p.m.

In the living room, Vesta and Franz wait for the livestream to start. *Today's the best day*, she says, pulling his snout closer. They kiss.

Earlier, a car came to pick her grandmother up. A man stepped out and opened the door, helping Vivienne into the backseat. Vesta noted that she was carrying no luggage, which meant she'd be back soon, as promised. Still, from the kitchen window, Vesta's stomach ached as she watched the black vehicle pull away. She'd begged Vivienne to take her along. But, *no dice*, as Lou had said. Velour and Lou, in the kitchen talking, have been treating Vesta like royalty. She even got to stay home from school today.

Nana's famous, she whispers, sitting on the giant red couch swinging her legs back and forth, feet not quite touching the floor.

She hears the grinding noise of teeth on teeth coming from . . . somewhere. She turns to face the basement door, then the bathroom door, then the other one at the top of three steps, the door that leads nowhere. But she cannot tell where it's originating.

Vesta isn't afraid of her home. Born in the upstairs bathroom, she's lived here since before she existed. It makes noises, confuses people. But is it, as she's heard Mackenzie's mother say, *cursed*?

No, Vesta concludes, studying the gallery scene on the video livestream. She squeals with joy, looks at Franz and says, *Christmas vacation.*

She's officially on Christmas break. Although she loves school, she's been dreading seeing Mackenzie. Pepper's black and white leg windmills into her thoughts, momentarily spinning away her good mood. Then, she feels a sudden rush of luck, for her own dog is still alive, heart beating beside her. She strokes Franz's hind leg, at least four times larger than Pepper's, and still connected to his body.

On the screen before her: a gallery in the New York City night filled with her grandmother's artwork. People are commenting, their words moving across the screen in real time, but Vesta is too far away to see what they're saying. She's waiting for her grandmother to walk into the frame. Last night, a variation on her usual dream:

Women in bonnets selling strudel and shoofly pies, old men eating hot dogs with buckets of sauerkraut on top, old men and women whose faces are melting off as they smile at little Vesta—four years old and miniature in dad's arms. Wearing a black sweater, dad only ever wears black—and today his skin is fast and clear like an angel's—Vesta knows her dad won't ever get old like these sauerkraut people— but she doesn't know how she knows—the duo walks through a long hallway lined with stalls—dad's clothes change from solid to lava—and Vesta's not wearing any at all—just water—and the hallway is not a hallway but a river flowing into the violent sea—the baubles and antiques the vendors are selling which Vesta finds quite pretty—bubblegum jewelry, glimmering junk, and bright old sweaters that reek of the dead start to float, drown. Dad's holding her—but his arms turn liquid—and over the whole scene—a dog—the dismembered body of a dog stuck in the sky like clouds over the beautiful ocean. The sky is evacuated of all constellations. Her father points up at the dog's bloody hind leg. That's the one, he says—the one you're named after. He smiles wide before telling her all about Cerberus, the three-headed dog of the underworld with claws. Look up again, he says—and the dog's three faces are the three fates—the fates which her grandmother has told her about—and they're weaving, spinning, and cutting—cutting up the dog—her father speaks with the voice of her Nana and says—there is the spinner, the allotter, and the cutter—the cutter is the most stubborn, determining when a human will die—unwavering, hard—then her dad barks . . .

~

She awoke this morning to Franz snarling out the window, at something in the field. When she looked, she couldn't see what was there—the fog thick and blue, hooking the dark green grass up with sky. Then, she rearranged her grandmother's old tarot cards: Queen of Swords, Three of Wands, Strength, Justice, Knight of Cups into a new configuration on her wall as she narrated her process to the dog. Vesta refers to this arranging and rearranging as *research*. She hears her mother use the word for nearly everything—Velour is always doing *research*. Do not disturb. On his lunch break, Lou had come home. Before Vivienne got into the car, Lou gave her a big kiss. Vesta guessed it must've been with tongue, because it was long and his head moved from side to side. Vesta and her mother watched. Later, upstairs, Lou told Vesta her room was like a museum. *Not really,* Vesta corrected, *in a museum you're not allowed to touch anything.* He pointed to *Tableau Vivant,* Vesta's favorite painting, where a giant fluffy dog embraces a naked woman. *This one puts me in a weird place,* said Lou. Vesta stepped back and considered the scene, then told him: *it's just a painting.* (Lou, so easily spooked!)

~

Vivienne walks into the frame, her black coat swaying.

Lars follows.

The gallery is lit bright and Vivienne looks ravishing, miniature, and buoyant in the wide white space, like she'll lift off the ground, start floating.

181

-Look! It's Nana! Vesta shrieks.

-She looks great, Velour says.

-Damn, Lou says, nodding.

Velour enlarges the video so that the comments from viewers watching at home, moving in a rapid blinky vertical line, are no longer visible and the three of them sit, transfixed. Vesta can see portions of the swarm of people standing before the building. Occasionally someone walks in front of the camera, blocking her view entirely.

-Are they *all* for Nana?

-Yes.

-Were you part of this crowd? Lou asks Velour.

-*Adjacent*.

-Mom *partied*, Vesta says, then moves closer to the screen.

Onscreen, Lars and Vivienne walk side by side, then stop and stand near one of the doll dresses.

To Vesta, it looks glamorous, scary, and alive—so much bigger, towering over her grandmother who sewed the thing so long ago.

Three loud taps at the door knock Vesta out of her zone.

Earlier, when Vesta took Franz on a walk downtown, Milo was standing at the town center, near the Christmas tree, smoking and holding an iced coffee. She'd nearly forgotten, until the knocks, that she'd invited him. Vesta fidgets with her brown velvet skirt, crumpling the material into soft balls.

-Vesta, you have a visitor, yells Velour.

Milo appears at the entrance to the living room, Velour behind him. Vesta takes a deep breath, pleasantly surprised to see him somewhere other than the street. Framed in the doorway: handsome body backlit by her very own kitchen.

-Hope it's cool I'm here.

-Hey man, Lou says.

The men nod at each other and Vesta watches their signals and ways. She imagines her father doing the same.

-You know him? Vesta asks.

-I went to high school with Milo, Lou says.

-Who *didn't* you go to high school with, Velour says.

-Vesta said you guys were having like, a party, Milo says.

-No! I didn't say that! Vesta says, shaking her head.

-Did too, Milo says, elbowing her.

She feels a jolt, and moves away from him.

-Vesta tends to be hyperbolic, Velour says.

Vesta can feel her face reddening. She tugs on her skirt, pulling the velvet down over her white tights, shrugging.

-That's my grandmother. In the gallery, the girl tells Milo.

-Oh shit. She looks awesome, Milo says, his hands folded on his lap, head bobbing. Vesta can see little flecks of dirt under his fingernails and his hands, which are thick and squishy as compared to the rest of his gaunt body, are bigger than both her dad's and Lou's. He's wearing a black t-shirt that says THIN LIZZY, a black velvety blazer with white stripes, and faded jeans. In the house, he looks skinnier than he does outside, even skinnier than her dad.

As Velour walks to the kitchen to get a smoke, she turns back and looks at her living room. Her mother and Lars are tiny on the screen, surrounded by Vivienne's soft sculptures—which Velour's never seen all together before: regal, performing, lit. She can almost smell where they came from, where she came from, cloth and thread packed with distant intel about whatever everyone was before.

Vivienne appears both ethereal and tough in her coat dress, lace stockings, and platform boots and Vesta's eyes are glued to her grandmother and Lars as they drift around the gallery floor mechanically, angels or robots. Franz is on her daughter's lap, his wide mouth smiling. Lou sits on one side of Vesta and Milo on the other, all of them stuck together as one meteoric and mineral bundle. She knows they are approaching the end. Can feel it in her chest.

-Those sculptures are *so sick*, Milo says, head bobbing. Milo is never totally still. His hands and feet twitch—making little spasmodic actions.

-*So sick*, Vesta repeats.

Lou laughs.

-Clothes for dolls? Milo asks.

-She made clothes for *my grandfather's* dolls, Vesta says.

-Big dolls, Milo says.

-Life-sized, Velour confirms, walking back into the living room, smoking.

Lou rolls his eyes and tells Milo that one of Hans's original dolls is in the basement.

-No shit! Milo exclaims.

-We don't really advertise it, Velour says, blowing a thin line of smoke in his face.

Silently, the four of them watch as Vivienne and Lars move around the gallery.

-What are they *doing*? asks Lou.

-Talking. Walking. Being watched, Velour says.

-I get that. But *why*?

-Prolly to get people talking, Milo says.

-Views and clicks, Velour says.

-Do you think she's happy? Lou asks, squinting at the screen.

-Hard to tell from here, Milo mutters.

-Yes! Vesta declares.

-Who is that guy though? Milo asks.

-The gallerist. *Lars*. Kind of an ass, Lou says.

-He's not an *ass*, Vesta says.

-No? Lou asks.

-I like him. His clothes are cool. Vesta says, swinging her legs.

-He looks pretty good, Milo says.

Vesta's heart pounds as she surveys the dudes. Lars is different from Lou and Lou is different from Milo and all of them are different from her dad. They're all the same, too. The girl's eyes well up. She's happy her grandmother is becoming a famous artist again, but she wishes *she* was strolling the fancy gallery. Wishes, too, that Milo was watching *her* on screen. She can easily imagine being seen that way. Milo is sitting beside her and he smells the way some guys smell: hazy, lemony, confusing.

She pictures herself in the space, surrounded by her *own* creations, on Lars Arden's arm. Her grandmother emanates a strange radiance which leaves the screen and travels through the room, infusing it with heat. The more radiant she looks, the more she disappears, disperses—taken by her own light. No longer earthly. Not exactly.

-Rad. To have a comeback, says Milo.

-She's at the peak of the dream of herself, I guess, Velour replies.

-Totally, Milo says.

-What the fuck does *that mean*? Lou asks.

Vesta giggles.

The room is filled with a demented tenderness. Vesta watches Lou regard her mother: intimate but distant, twitchy. Then, she watches her mother watch her own mother.

Suddenly, Velour's features freeze and Vesta's stomach twists.

Something's happened on screen. This is Velour's *bad news* face, the face Vesta hates most, so she instinctually closes her eyes and strokes Franz over and over.

She can almost hear crickets in the field—the field next door or those fields her grandmother says souls go, depending on whether they were good, bad, or somewhere in the middle.

Vesta can't remember what they're called.

Those fields.

Wool and silk coverings for nubs, a set of trousers with four legs.

Bra with one cup, thread everywhere, thread connecting the living to the dead.

Turns to her left. Milo's face is frozen like her mother's. To her right, Lou. His expression strange, new.

On screen, Vivienne is in the center of the room surrounded by people-like mannequins and dress forms inside a grotesque wardrobe. They crowd her, enclosing her body, which has fallen to the floor.

Velour, Lou, and Milo all look to Vesta.

The music stops.

Her grandmother is horizontal, squiggly. There's a brick on the floor beside her and the window's gone except for broken shards. Nothing separates the throng of people from Vivienne and Lars.

A pool of red spreads along the floor.

Vesta badly wants her own doll. She'd like to take care of it.

Where is it?

She moves a loose tooth around with her tongue, back and forth, back and forth as Franz leaps off the couch and Velour gathers her daughter in her arms.

Vesta tastes blood as she pushes it up and in, up and in—trying to re-root the loose tooth.

Lou whisks the laptop away and Vesta can feel hands and paws in her hair.

Her mother, Milo, Lou, Franz.

Where?

Velour, satin, silk, tornado-gray wool.

Gone!

Velour rocks Vesta back and forth. Someone's crying, but Vesta's not sure who. The image of her grandmother on the floor of the gallery with Lars hunched over her is no longer there.

In its place, a black field with white type:

YOUR VIDEO WILL RESUME SOON

Mozart's *Eine Kleine Nachtmusik* playing.

Nervous, fast-paced tunes soothe Vesta.

A little of the cure in the poison, as she'd heard her grandmother say.

A little night music, a little night music, a little night music, music in the night—

YOUR VIDEO WILL RESUME SOON

HOLD TIGHT

~

Vesta wakes up to a blur of bright lights. Velour and Franz are asleep next to her on the couch and there's a slow moaning sound. She rubs her eyes and the little multicolored bulbs stuck into the miniature white ceramic Christmas tree in the middle of the living room come into focus. She smiles. She'd been asking her mother to set the Christmas tree up—and it's finally done. The music slows—but Vesta still can't tell where it's coming from. She wakes her mother up and points to the small ceramic tree.

-We put it up while you were sleeping, Velour says.

Then, she remembers.

-Is she dead? Vesta asks.

~

It was supposed to snow but it's not cold enough.

So, rain. Damp branches make muted taps against the windowpane as Lou packs the car. Velour, Vesta, and Franz leave the house and walk to the edge of the yard where the wind whistles and strings.

In the field, Vesta feels exposed, in danger, thrilled—as though anything, anyone, anything, anyone—could swoop.

The sky rises bright blue over the black grass.

Velour holds her daughter. Franz follows.

When they get to the middle, they stop moving and the motion detector light shines on them as the rain falls in horizontal streaks.

When next she wakes, Vesta is dry and moving in the backseat of the car, surrounded by city.

VIVIENNE

December 20

6:00 p.m.

Gallery X

A bright flash of light overtakes the space, making the gallery imageless for an instant: one of Vivienne's visions. Vivienne and Lars stand at the entrance to the gallery near the square window separating them from the night and people. Lars asks if he can get her anything. A camera, somewhere, capturing them. *We're live, Vivienne*, says Lars. She stares out at the crowd. The mass of faces is familiar, like it's always been here, waiting for her to arrive. She doesn't recognize anyone in particular, but the way they move together as a swarm, she *knows*. A man mouths something. He stands beside a woman in a red hat. She can't make out the silent words. Maybe: *do you remember me?* She waves, then turns away. A homeless man carries a red umbrella and mirrors her. When she moves, he moves too.

Years ago, while sewing the doll clothes, she was pregnant with Velour and the flashes of light—the visions—increased. They knocked her over. Pinned to the ground by a painful and ecstatic light she hoped was sent by God's celestial arms, she decided to stop. Just, *stop*. She began sewing clothes for other people, moving around with her young daughter, and attending church.

She looks up at Lars. Even in heeled boots, she's at least five inches shorter than him. For the occasion, she's wearing lace tights and extra makeup—blush, concealer, dark red-purple lipstick. Her gray hair, in a pile on top of her head, shakes as Vivienne looks back at the throng: red hat, red umbrella, clusters of black jackets huddled together on the last day of autumn.

Lars is speaking in soft whispers, reiterating, as if she's senile, that this event is a soft opening, a preview before the hard opening in a week, and that if she doesn't like the way things look, how her work interacts with the space, anything, they can change it. Nothing is permanent. The public hasn't arrived yet. *But the public is already here,* Vivienne thinks. *Can they hear us? No. No sound, just image. It's very calm. It'll be just like this. The whole time, just like this. Walking around and around.*

They approach a crinoline cage dress with a wooly blouse of intestines, a red sewn pony and black and white dog between the dress form and the fabric, one of the last doll garments she made.

I made this one after he died. I was so pregnant I was about to burst. I'm not sure why I put the animals there—all the insides are on the outside and the outsides, in.

Vivienne can hear a garbage truck, metal mechanical force moving in the night, overtaking the crowd.

Lars hovers near her, nervous, a small bead of sweat forming on his forehead which she wipes away with an embroidered handkerchief.

She thinks he might cry. Vivienne is calm, statuesque.

The light's almost gone, its final pops like firework duds against a pitch sky.

They continue walking.

Vivienne reaches out to touch one of the pieces and Lars intervenes. When the NAT asked for her sculptures a few months ago, she had Velour ship them as-is. The garments had been at rest in that basement for years near *The Machine-Gunneress.* Now they're visible—propped up, almost foreign. Their presence in the house was somehow important to Velour, and she was sad to see them go. Vivienne, on the other hand, was relieved to release them. She turns back, studying the soundless crowd.

The doll's wardrobe is energized, emitting wafts of her other life: the five years after Wilma jumped and before Velour was born—when she made these things, when it was just her and Hans.

They approach a dress made from clear plastic and pink felt. The pink felt is meant to run along the length of a spine. The gallery people have chosen to display it as a chaotic mass on the floor, crumpled like shed skin. One could almost walk by it, an afterthought. Vivienne points and nods approvingly. Lars smiles.

Vivienne turns to the people. The light redacts them, and then her. So dazzled—nothing. She stops walking. Turns back to her work. Blinks, rubs her eyes, blinks.

When Lars looks down at his phone, she feels her body must be inside his device, ether and screen, a blurred almost-figure emanating scab-colored light. She can feel Velour, Lou, and Vesta watching from far away.

The muscular, fashionable curator with a smooth head mutates into a young Hans Bellmer. She smiles and throws her arms around his neck.

Vivienne looks down at the bright white ground and, facing the dazzling and decrepit scraps of past, hears shattering glass. Her head—now totally clear—throbs.

She gazes up at the ceiling, her mouth gaping.

Beads of rain pour down on her, clear and sharp.

She can hear a voice, faint. Hans?

A stranger stands beside her, above her—*no, no, no.*

Soft satin ribbons hang down from the man's coat and graze Vivienne's face.

A stud of light dilates, then overtakes.

LARS

December 20

Evening

The moans of the city and a siren so loud and vibratory it could be coming from inside his own chest cavity. This is Lars's first time in the back of an ambulance—dodging traffic like they're in a video game someone else, someone far away, is playing.

His clammy palm encloses the old woman's hand, cold and skeletal.

When the paramedic, a laconic, capable man much younger than him, asks if he is Vivienne's son, Lars pauses.

Static comes through the radio clasped to the medic's shoulder, covering the only question Lars can think to ask—*is she going to make it?*

He tries to funnel all his attention into the twin plastic tubes shooting oxygen up her nostrils, to enter a meditation.

As he strokes her hair and stares into the tubes, Lars's phone dings. Behind his phone, lit with texts, Vivienne's bloody head.

GALLERY X GROUP TEXT

CLORINDA 6:47 pm
how is she?
is she okay??

LARS 6:47 pm
WHAT THE FUCK
Sd;flkjekrjlskjfldjfsdfksslkdf2

SIXTINE 6:47 pm
that was NOT our brick

LARS 6:48 pm
i didn't fucking signal
i did not wave
i said NO TSUTN
*NO STUNT

RONI 6:38 pm
NOT OUR BRICK
we still have our brick

LARS 6:48 pm
ANOTHER BRICK?
WHO?

SIXTINE 6:48 pm
we dunno
no one saw

Fucking breathing. How is it possible no one saw? The event was being recorded! Soul not gone yet. She just needs to rest. Be a fucking man. Call Velour, Lou, Vesta. Vesta. Tell the crew to draft a statement. How to frame it?

Suddenly, he's running alongside a moving bed holding Vivienne's hand.

Someone fastens a paper bracelet to his wrist which reads EMERGENCY ROOM ONLY. Across his FUCK knuckle tattoo, a splatter of the artist's blood. He tries to keep up, goes faster, can't feel his legs, trips. *Careful, sir!*

CLORINDA 6:48 pm
everyone talking about this
Viv is blowing up

RONI 6:49 pm
FYI
ALL pieces SOLD

SIXTINE 6:49 pm
how is she?

CLORINDA 6:50 pm
L how r u
holding up?
remember NOT your fault

RONI 6:50 pm
up until the brick
the night was so chill

SIXTINE 6:50 pm
we wld never be so careless
some fucker WANTED to knock her out

CLORINDA 6:51 pm
LARS?
maybe no signal at hospital

RONI 6:52 pm
reporter is here
asking abt Viv

LARS 7:02 pm
DELETE ALL THIS

REMOVAL

SVETLANA
@Sweatlana

VIVIENNE VOLKER LITERALLY JUST GOT HIT WITH A BRICK AT
@GALLERYX SOMEONE TELL ME WHAT IS HAPPENING
6:27pm   December 20
39 shares   **107** likes

GALLERY X
@galleryxnyc

The wonderful artist Vivienne Volker
is being treated at NYU Medical Center.
Prayers to her and her loved ones.
7:32pm   December 20
201 shares   **903** likes

**IDENTIFIED SURREALIST OBJECT:
CONTROVERSIAL ARTIST VIVIENNE VOLKER
STRUCK BY A BRICK
AS OVER 3,000 WATCH ON LIVESTREAM**

**ALL 27 'SHOCKING AND TENDER SCULPTURAL
GARMENTS FOR MUTILATED DOLLS' HAVE SOLD,
SAYS LARS ARDEN,
GALLERY X OWNER
THE SHOW OFFICIALLY OPENS
TO THE PUBLIC
DECEMBER 27th**

**ONLOOKERS 'TRAUMATIZED'
IN THE WAKE OF DRAMA
AT VIVIENNE VOLKER PREVIEW
ON MANHATTAN'S LOWER EAST SIDE
'GLASS. BLOOD. A NIGHTMARE.'
'THE BRICK CAME FROM NOWHERE'**

@JesusisLord8181 3 hours ago
PRAY FOR HER
LORD & SAVIOR

@lit7703 3 hours ago
did anyone see who did it?
i was in a trance

@heyfivebux 3 hours ago
she dead

@systemprocessings 3 hours ago
i threw the brick ✍

@user6652001 3 hours ago
i threw the brick

@anonb8 3 hours ago
i threw the brick!!!

@dressedinf1nitud3 3 hours ago
go troll some other world asshole

@lit7703 3 hours ago
was mad cinematic

VELOUR

December 21

Morning

FALL RISK reads the paper band wrapped around her mother's wrist. Vesta fidgets with the bracelet and strokes Vivienne's arm, tracing a shadowy purple vein. *You'll be okay,* the girl whispers before pressing her cheek against her grandmother's hand.

-Is she in heaven, you think?

-She's unconscious. Sleeping.

-I *know* that. I'm talking about Pepper.

-Pepper . . . Velour's mind is blank.

-Pepper! The dog! Vesta shouts.

-Oh right. Pepper's in heaven. For sure.

-You really think?

-I don't know, Vest. But yes, I suspect.

Velour sighs, surprised at how peaceful she feels as she scans her mother's body. Shut down. Closed. Not dead. No. But not speaking, either. A phantasm. The hospital TV plays mute news, a closed caption scrolling along the bottom:

**WINTER SOLSTICE, SHORTEST DAY OF THE
YEAR, LONGEST NIGHT THE 17 BEST TYPES
OF CHRISTMAS LIGHTS ARTIST IN CRITICAL
CONDITION AFTER BEING STRUCK BY BRICK
BABY KANGAROO GOES VIRAL FOR DANCING
LIKE FRED ASTAIRE**

Her mother's hand, prehistoric and papery inside Vesta's pink fleshy one. She sees Pepper's stiff hind leg, Vesta cradling it just before Lars pulled up a few days ago. She'd been so wrong about how Pepper would meet her end. She didn't see the hawk coming. Not really. Or did she? Did she see this coming? A brick to her mother's head. Vivienne lying unconscious as people blather. Velour yearns for quiet. Some voices mourning, others rejoicing, humming, stammering. The constant chatter melts all speech into a glue which sticks to Velour, viscous and outlandish, a discourse hardening around her. Somewhere in the gummy delirium, silence.

And what about Velour?

-It's gonna be okay, she tells her daughter, wincing at her own words, which feel wrong. Better to say nothing, maybe. To stop speaking entirely. Still, she's heard other mothers, mothers in television shows and movies, make such impossible pledges to their children. Vesta raises an eyebrow.

-Promise? Vesta asks.

-Yes.

-Nana! Vesta shrieks.

-What?

-I hear her!

Velour is too tired to refute.

-What's she saying? The child presses her ear against Vivienne's forehead and Velour looks into her small paper cupful of hospital coffee, then back down at her mother's blue FALL RISK bracelet, which matches the color of the gown they've put her in—dry and disposable and sky-colored, though the sky is presently a grimy white, the exact color of Velour's house. The first rays of winter sun are struggling to shove through the opaque cloud, pathetic.

In the antiseptic glow, Vivienne's wrinkles and lines are visible under her smeared makeup. She looks her age, almost. Vesta's on one side of the mechanical bed, Velour's on the other, and a window behind them is filled in with open sky. Sixteenth floor. Vesta rests her hand on her grandmother's tangle of hair.

Velour puts Vivienne's coat on and buttons it all the way up, the way her mother does. It fits.

-Can you still hear her? Velour asks.

-She's *cold*, Vesta says, nodding.

Lou has gone to get doughnuts, per Vesta's request. Velour wonders, again, if fate or God is playing sick cosmic tricks on her while she watches Vesta comb Vivienne's hair. Her eyes wander back to the paper bracelet. She wonders, too, what part she's played in her mother getting hit. FALL RISK. She gazes at her mother until she obscures into a smudge of blue.

The sun brightens the room as it sputters through white and Velour wishes for two or three splashes of whiskey and a cigarette. From outside, the three women look uncannily alike through the institution's window. Vesta and Velour in matching long black coats, puffy sleeves and custom buttons handsewn by Vivienne Volker, and Viv between them: small and stunned and surrounded by multicolored Christmas lights.

~

Lars Arden, in the same black getup he donned last night on the livestream, enters the hospital room and approaches Vivienne, shaky.

-Doesn't she look a little better? Velour asks.

-We should've protected her. We still don't know who threw it. Theories are circulating, Lars says.

-Theories? Velour asks.

-Some say it was performance art.

-How grotesque.

-Grotesque, Vesta repeats.

-Other footage may surface. Some audience members were filming.

-Please. Let's stop talking, Velour says.

They sit in silence around Vivienne as Velour replays her own conception story, as relayed by her mother while she was manically happy, not long after receiving word that she would be the only living artist to appear in the NAT Museum's show. Velour—made from Hans's final nut—a last days baby.

Velour takes the final cold swig of coffee then runs her hand over the white wall. Her mother and daughter like two automatons sleepwalking through a long hall, hair freshly combed. Velour runs her hand over her own hair: matted, stringy.

Lars stares out the window into the gray.

-Velour, says Lars, *every* motherfucking piece sold.

Vesta smiles at Lars, still combing her grandmother's hair.

-You're the executor of the estate, right?

-Right.

-Can I paint Nana's nails? Vesta asks.

-Sure.

Velour takes three bottles of nail polish out of a suitcase she'd packed in a mad rush before they left for New York. She'd shoved everything she could find into the bag. Vesta's eyes sparkle as she snatches the bottles—pink, black, green. She sets them on the table next to her grandmother's head and steps back, regarding them from afar. She moves closer to Lars, then back toward Vivienne—pacing. Finally, she begins painting, alternating the colors. She does the same to her own nails as she whispers something into Vivienne's ear which Velour cannot hear. Lars watches, transfixed, as though he's been hit.

～

In the hospital bathroom, Velour mistakes herself for her mother. She models the coat in the mirror, turning around. In one of the pockets, a handkerchief embroidered VV. Now that she's away from the house, she can smell the stale smoke and dust and perfume of that place—the coat is caked with it. She waves the hanky through the air like a fake ghost as she flashes to last Sunday when Vivienne, Velour, and Vesta were sitting in the kitchen. Her own home suddenly foreign.

I had a terrible dream.
Me too!
What was yours, mon cherie?
Dog hanging from tree.
Like the movie we watched.
What movie?
Why not? Nothing too bad in there.
Just dogs hanging from trees.
It didn't make me sad. I liked the movie.
What does morbid mean?
Try to figure it out.
What was your dream, Mom?
I don't remember. But I woke up, you know, in a horrid psychic residue.
Put your damn coat on.

Velour shoves the handkerchief back into her mother's pocket. As she pees, she gets wonderfully empty.

Her period, over.

Her mother, resting.

Money, coming.

She looks at herself again, smirking before leaving. Back in the room, she observes Vesta reaching for Lars's hand, their fingers lying entwined atop Vivienne. They remain like this for some time. Vesta turns to her grandmother and whispers, then presses her ear against her stomach.

I'm not Vivienne, not anymore, not really. Vivienne's over there, wearing her coat.

The old woman's arm lifts up in one sweeping, graceful motion as though she's dancing. All stare, entranced, at the moving limb, its freshly painted nails, before it comes to rest again on the bed. Velour returns to the bedside.

-What was *that*? asks Velour

-Does that mean she'll wake up?

-Maybe, Lars tells Vesta.

-She's *cold*, Vesta insists, gritting her teeth.

-Look through the suitcase. Pick something out for her.

-Is that a vintage Vivienne Westwood? asks Lars, pointing to the bag.

Vesta blows on her small fingernails and touches them, ensuring they're dry before diving into the garments as Lars watches.

-Beautiful! she exclaims, holding up a white satin robe embroidered with birds.

-Do you think she killed anybody? asks Vesta, dropping one of the frocks on Lars's lap.

Lars shrugs, a tear streaming down his cheek.

Vesta hums.

Lou appears at the door.

-Only three people can be in here with her at once, says Velour.

-I can go, Lars says.

-You can stay until they make you leave, Velour says.

Lou sits down and Lars stands beside the bed, behind the girl. The three adults watch as the child dresses the dying artist. Vesta whispers into her ear, then listens and nods, as though she's having a conversation with her Nana. She bends Vivienne's arm before sending it carefully through the sleeve, smoothing the bunched fabric around her shoulder. Velour props Vivienne up as Vesta wraps the robe around her back. Velour takes over, maneuvering Vivienne's arm into the other sleeve.

They lay her back down on the bed and Vesta covers the blue hospital gown with the white robe.

AFTERLIFE

VESTA & LARS

11 years later

Mojave Desert

The sky's flat blue, its air blowing hot against Vesta's face. Since entering the desert, the landscape's been the same cracked beige. She zones out watching from the passenger's seat. Repeat repeat repeat. She doesn't know how long they've been driving through this scenery. It's like the placeless place where images and dreams get made before they're sent down into minds to circulate. Where the end affixes itself to the beginning. It's late summer. When they arrive at their destination, Vesta will see Vivienne for the first time in years.

-How much longer? Vesta asks.

-Twenty minutes or so. Maybe less, Lars replies, stroking her hair which blows across the car and into his face—long, stringy, dirty blonde. All windows open.

-There's nothing here. Do you think it's just gonna pop up, out of nowhere?

-That's how your mom described it.

-Don't talk about my mom to me.

-Sorry.

-And don't say sorry.

-Sorry.

-What are you gonna do while they're screening me?

-Wander around, I guess. Wait.

-Will you stay close? she asks.

-Of course. Read me the brochure?

-*Again?* You're insane, Vesta says, laughing.

She squeezes his hand, then rummages through the glove compartment: candy, maps, costume jewelry, cigarettes, papers, tickets. She opens the brochure, which flaps in the wind, and clears her throat. On the cover, an image of a cloudless blue sky, identical to the one which now envelops them. She begins to read loudly over the dry breeze. Lars almost closes his eyes.

The Center for Constant Creation [CCC]
An Undisclosed Location in the Mojave Desert

The Center for Constant Creation is a retreat center and arts collective located on five acres of dreamy desert landscape and funded by the Voortelle Corporation and the United States government. Our mission is two-fold.

- First, we seek to deliver productive and purposeful afterlives to those in persistent vegetative states so that their bodies may remain creative and useful long after they've stopped legally living.
- Second, our work transforms the often unnecessarily messy and risky process of creating new life. By taking reproduction out of the hands of chance and into the luxury of our desert facility, the CCC fosters safety and equity, while de-emphasizing the role of capricious and often harmful nature.

Here at the Center, we are artists and language-workers. We believe words and we believe in words. Terminology creates a vision for the future we want to see. As such, we call our comatose birthers *artists* and the birthing process *collaboration*. With our roots in non-hierarchical decision making, the CCC prioritizes the care of our artists and staff as we collaborate on the exciting process of creating the future.

The CCC was the first birthing center of its
kind and we are thrilled that new centers
are popping up every year, each with its own
character, look, and feel.

Our chic yet cozy facility consists of two
ultramodern abodes:

- The Studio, wherein a cohort of artists
  collaborate with our staff on the
  gestation of the next generation.
- The Office, for all social and
  administrative functions.

With our mid-century modern decor and 1:1
artist-collaborator ratio, there is *nothing*
institutional about our bright, open, and
hands-on facility. The breathtaking high
desert location is home to famously psychedelic
sunsets, oneiric winds, pinyon pines, Juniper,
and a fluffy Flemish Giant rabbit named
Britomart, our resident therapy bunny.

*Note: While entrance to The Studio requires
security clearance, interested visitors may
make an appointment to stop by The Office and
chat with a member of the collective.

Our inaugural cohort entered the Center in
March of 2024. Among them was Vivienne Volker,
an eighty-two-year-old female-identifying
artist who had been in a persistent coma
for three months and was declared brain

dead. Her daughter, Velour Bellmer, signed
Volker into our care on March 21, 2024.
Despite her advanced age, Volker's womb was
remarkably viable and capable of withstanding
multiple tests which advanced our research
tremendously. Vivienne has enjoyed an
astounding run of nearly eleven peaceful and
productive years here at the CCC, where we
collaborated on four innovative and successful
pregnancies together. Indeed, due to her
enormous legacy, Volker's was one of our most
sought after and poetically hospitable wombs.

As her tenure comes to a close, the time has
come to say goodbye to Vivienne. The collective
mourns and rejoices. Her final art project was
completed last year, at age ninety-two, when
she became the oldest womb owner (conscious
or unconscious) to carry a child to term. It
was a truly magical experience welcoming baby
C (we keep full names and parental identities
confidential) into the world, reinforcing our
shared vision of a future bright with pregnancy
(and creation of every sort) that is without
strife. Volker has been a marvelous host, and
we are confident that we've returned the favor
in kind. Bravo to all involved.

Vivienne's imminent departure means that we'll
have one space open in our comfortable seven-
room facility, and that we are currently taking
applications for those who meet the criteria.

-I love your voice. You *know* someone from the art world helped write that, Lars says, I wonder who it was.

In the distance, two pink buildings rise. Vesta's heart pounds. Before she's allowed entrance into the studio to see her grandmother, she must get cleared by one of the collective members. A man stands outside the smaller of the two buildings, waving languidly his whole arm as they approach. Vesta squints into the sun. Sitting on the porch beside the waving man, the biggest bunny she's ever seen. Vesta looks at Lars, tears filling her eyes.

-I guess *that's* the guy, Vesta says, pointing.

-What's he *wearing*? Just be calm. And they'll let you in.

-Really?

-Of course. You're not *dangerous*.

-I don't even know what they want, though.

As Vesta steps out of the car, Lars grabs her clothes the way he sometimes does, pulling her into him. They're both in all black and Vesta is wearing her grandmother's old coat, worn and baggy, over her plain black tank top and shorts. On her feet, Vivienne's platform boots—the ones she was wearing when the brick hit. Vesta crouches down and pets the rabbit, who flops over onto his side, catatonic and showing his belly.

The man introduces himself as Dean Konig. He tells Lars that he can explore the grounds while waiting, and that their conversation is not likely to last for more than an hour. Vesta picks up the bunny, stroking its hot fur on the concrete porch as wind blows up her coat. She asks if she can bring the animal into the office for their conversation. Dean shakes his head and Vesta places the rabbit down, then steps into the office: open and circular and lined with windows.

From here, the desert looks eternal, terrifying. Vesta spins around, trying to figure out from which direction they entered. She eyes Dean, a semi-handsome tan man with dark hair, wearing white pants and a shirt made from, she guesses, something like hemp, a long white smock overtop, hands resting in pockets. They sit down in a pair of white womb chairs, facing each other. Dean presses RECORD.

VESTA FURIO TRANSCRIPT

Vesta Furio (18) arrived early this morning
(September 19, 2035) via car from Pennsylvania
with her husband, Lars Arden (48) in order to
say goodbye to Vivienne. Per CCC protocol, Furio
consented to participate in a recorded conversation
with Dean Konig (36), trusted collective member and
Volker's longtime collaborator. The conversation
was a chance for the collective to get to know
Furio and to hear how she regards our work here at
the Center so that we might come to an informed
decision about whether or not she poses any threats
to our work and reputation.

After reviewing the transcript, and after much
discussion, it is the collective's decision that
Furio's security clearance be denied. We feel her
entrance into The Studio may disrupt the artists and
staff. We also feel (more crucially) that The Studio
may disrupt her own mental health, which appears
to be quite fragile, if not seriously disturbed. We
submit the below transcript for your review.

VESTA FURIO: Why the old-fashioned tape recorder?

DEAN KONIG: We find that it's comforting to people,
              its clunky visibility. One of our
              major things here is transparency.
              Keeping things out in the open.
              Digital technology feels more hidden,
              secretive.

V: But you use computers.

D: When we have to. Now let me begin by—

V: Did you write the literature on this place?

D: We did it together. Collectively.

V: Do you have a boss?

D: We try to be non-hierarchical.

V: So you don't have a boss.

D: I didn't say that.

V: How did you get into this stuff?

D: I wanted to be at the forefront of something. I was always good with people. My own mother was sickly and I had to care for her from a young age.

V: Do you live here?

D: Yep.

V: At the forefront.

D: Right. Is he okay out there? [Lars Arden was walking around the perimeter of the office and had begun to pace.]

V: Yeah. This is basically our honeymoon. Funny, huh.

D: Is this your first time in the desert?

V: The literal desert, yes.

D: You drove from Pennsylvania? You don't fly.

V: I don't.

D: Not ever?

V: Never.

D: Can I ask why?

V: I doubt humans are supposed to be up there. That high. Do you think I'll get clearance? What's the protocol?

D: No formal protocol, per se. But, after we talk, the collective will review the transcript. Then, Voortelle will clear you for entrance. Or not.

V: And if 'or not?'

D: We'll cease life support without your presence.

V: So she'll die alone? What the fuck.

D: Not alone, no. I'll be there.

V: How is she?

D: You've seen our updates, right?

V: Yes, but it's always hard to tell in photos. And they seem staged.

D: They're candid, I assure you. I think she's held up quite well. I take care of her.

V: What do you mean?

D: Sponge baths, exercises, outdoor time, reading, companionship.

V: Right. You advertise her womb as 'poetically hospitable . . .'

D: We don't really see our language as *advertising*. It's a self-selecting process. Are you thinking of having a baby?

V: Is that one of the questions you're supposed to ask me? I don't want a baby.

D: There aren't prescribed questions. This is just a conversation. Not an interrogation. How would you describe your years, the ones since Vivienne entered the Center?

V: [silence] I don't know. *Waiting.* I just want to see her. You know, I heard her voice. We had a conversation. Before they shipped her here.

D: Vivienne? [long silence] A conversation? What did she say? [clears throat]

V: It was like her voice had been stripped of all its plaque. There was no filter. It was frightening, but under the fear, I grasped what was happening. Not with my mind. With something else. The first thing I heard her say was 'I'm not Vivienne, not anymore, not really. Vivienne's over there, wearing her coat.' And I understood she was talking about my mother. My mother was wearing my grandmother's coat at the time, which I found odd. It's actually *this* coat. I'm wearing it now.

D: So you really believe she spoke to you?

V: I could hear her circling around an afterlife— for whatever reason, in that dark electric arena between the end and the beginning, like a glitch after the catastrophe of the brick.

D: Did you talk to her? Could she hear you?

V: I don't know. We seemed to be having a conversation, but it was unlike any conversation I'd ever had.

D: [silence] Can you describe it in further detail?

V: It belies description. Surreal. Ha!

D: You realize this may impact your security clearance. I just want to be fully transparent. Because you claim to have heard her . . . *voice* . . .

V: Shit. What? Can we scratch that, then. Do you mind if I light this?

D: There's no smoking in here.

V: Even if I could describe it, I'm not sure I'd tell you. I mean, why would I?

D: What you're saying is problematic. I want you to be able to be with your grandmother at the end. You are family, after all. And that's important. But . . .

V: I remember dressing my grandmother in her clothing, clothing I'd never seen her wear before. Her arms were heavy but limp. You do all that, right? Dress her . . .

D: I do.

V: Do you ever do anything untoward?

D: *Untoward?*

V: To the patients.

D: What? Of course not. And we call them *artists*.

V: Are they all pregnant?

D: Not all. Some of them are resting. Between projects.

V: Oh. Yeah. The way you've decorated this place. It's kind of retro-futurist. I grew up in a different kind of place.

D: How do you mean?

V: An old farmhouse. Rickety, lots of hidden spaces. Here, everything's smooth. My parents were real romantic about the country. Mom still lives there, but you know that.

D: Why were they romantic about the country?

V: Because they grew up in cities. My father in New York, and my mother all over—Paris, Berlin. Vivienne couldn't just *sit*, so she moved them around a lot. On the contrary, that's all my mother does.

D: Sit?

V: Yes. She's like the sun making all the planets fall into her orbit. Or, not the sun. A faraway star. A fixed star. Further out.

D: She's bright.

V: And distant. Appears still. But, she's always moving, making moves.

D: When she visits Vivienne here, she seems quite warm, actually. What do you think of the drawings your mother made?

V: Her drawings of my comatose pregnant grandmother? I was moved by them, we both were. Lars showed them at the gallery, you know. Mom is dubious but I like her art. She really captured her mother.

D: I agree. The drawings are astonishing. And, well, your mother let you come here. To be with Vivienne when we take her off the machine. That's something.

V: She can't deal with shit like this. She wanted her to stay alive forever. Well, not alive. But not dead.

D: When did you marry Lars?

V: That's not one of the questions, is it?

D: Again, this isn't scripted. I'm winging it.

V: We got married on my 18th birthday. A few days ago.

D: Congratulations. And you came *here* right away?

V: Of course. I'm of age now. We bought a house, too. With Vivienne money, actually. It was built in 1968. The same year the term *brain death* was coined. Ha!

D: Is that right?

V: Brain death, irreversible coma. Death by neurological criteria. I could hear my grandmother. Though, I don't know if I'd call them *thoughts*. What I heard. Thinking is rare, even among the legally living. Right? Maybe it was a miracle. That's what she'd say. What are you looking at?

D: Nothing. You . . . you look like her. It's striking. What else?

V: When it comes to the brain, science is baffled. I think my mother's drawings show Vivienne's spark. Essence, whatever. They tell on this place.

D: You don't approve of what we do?

V: [silence] Am I supposed to answer honestly? I can't tell if I'm really supposed to be transparent or not. I just want to see my grandmother.

D: Good. Yeah. We just want to know what you think. Best to be honest. It seems you disagree with us. With our work.

V: [silence] I think we're always collaborating with the dead. But there's something godless— or maybe that's Vivienne speaking—about how you guys do it. [Gazed out the window, waved at Lars Arden, who was outside looking at The Office.] It's like he can't see me.

D: He can't. The windows are mirrors.

V: What's he looking at now? [Lars was looking at the ground, crouched over.]

D: Intestines, I'm guessing. Something left them behind earlier. Ate the whole animal and left those.

V: Any other questions? May I see her?

D: What made you fall in love with your husband?

V: You want me to describe love? I met him when I was quite young.

D: Did you love him then?

V: In my soul, I guess.

D: You believe in a soul?

V: Sure. Maybe it was my grandmother's *soul* that spoke. I don't know.

D: Do you think our artists' souls are still here?

V: I don't know. Maybe I could tell if I entered The Studio. It's kind of a pretty building. Lars is right near The Studio door. I guess he can't see in there, though.

D: It's impossible to see in. Those windows are mirrors, too. What was it about Lars that so moved you?

V: That's your best question yet. He seemed to grasp me. Something hallucinatory. And, he's handsome. [Looked out the window again.]

D: You're saying you *hallucinate*? Could it be that Vivienne's voice—what you *thought* you heard— was a hallucination?

V: I think most people do, no? Hallucinate. At least a little. The CCC's language about the afterlife. Did you come up with that?

D: Not me. All of us. The collective.

V: Schopenhauer said after you die you'll be what you were before you were born.

D: Are you pro-life?

V: I'm pro-afterlife. Although, I don't know if
this place is really what my grandmother had
in mind. [Silence] I feel like she was a bird
who became a dog. [Note: At this point, Furio's
speech became nonsensical. She began looking out
the window in a kind of trance, moving her head
slowly from side to side.]

D: What? A bird . . .

V: The gizzard grinds down food. A second stomach.
A second moon. [Furio looked completely dazed
at this point, absent.] Sirens, oxygen in
twin streams shooting up the nose, sparkling
garments, the snow still holding.

D: I'm not sure what you are referring to.

V: [She now appeared more lucid, as though she
had come to, and began making eye contact with
me again.] There was one moment, a moment when
I *knew* I'd never see her awake again. It was
shortly after I watched her get struck. I was
in the living room with Lou, my mom, and Milo.
The dog, too. On screen. Weird to see something
like that. I was a little kid. And I didn't
know shit. But I knew she'd somehow given her
life to art. Or art took her life. Or, it had
nothing much to do with art—whatever that trash
can of a word means—and more to do with evil.
Anonymous, boring. A thick dense red brick.
That image kept replacing the embryo in my

head. Do you know that piece? My grandfather's
drawing? It's called *The Red Embryo*. Kind of
swirly. In the embryo, an old woman, bloody.
Where was the embryo? The old woman? My
grandfather? My mother? Anyway, Milo sat beside
me. My grandmother had gone to church, had
eaten the body of Christ, all that stuff, the
day before. After it happened, I fell asleep.
I must've conked out from the blow, like that
embryonic brick bonked *me*, changing *my* brain.
I'm rambling. [silence . . . long exhale] But Lou
was packing the car. Lou was my grandmother's
boyfriend. As you know, my mother and him
are together. Such a soap opera. Anyway, we
stood there in the side yard—God I love that
property—the moon was full and the motion
detector light switched on. Suddenly, we were
spotlit under it. Went *click, click* . . . [long
exhale] That's how I remember it. Only, I don't
think we *had* one of those lights. I doubt we
did. I envied kids who had new houses with lots
of contraptions and stuff. Anyway, we stood
under a bright blue light and the field was black
and the wind got stringy but strong and began
to whistle and blow. I felt naked, super-porous
like the way they talk about medieval girls,
madly open to whatever and the wind had a wing
and the wing swept me. I could feel the gizzard
digesting me. It was like the middle of the
labyrinth, the part where the animal or God or
whoever . . . eats you. Wind and stomach and the
wall that blocks and supports it all. The rain

was falling but it was falling the wrong way. Not vertical. Horizontal. Like Van Gogh. Then, everything got very slow—too slow—all of us—on screen and off—trudging through sludge towards oblation. But I was already there.

D: [clears throat] And that's when you knew she wouldn't wake up?

V: Yep. [Furio appeared to zone out again. Looked past me at nothing.]

D: Are you still here?

V: Do you think they'll let me in?

D: I wish I could tell you. I'm not sure. It will take some time to arrive at consensus. You and I are almost done.

V: How do you know?

ACKNOWLEDGEMENTS

Thank you to my husband, Michael Newton, for his mad love and beyond brilliant editorial feedback. Thanks also to my parents and brother for their warmth, support, and hilarity. I am grateful for Stephan Zguta at Arcade for his kindness and for providing me with the best publishing experience I've ever had. Endless thanks, also, to Tony Lyons, Rachel Marble, and everyone at Arcade for their generosity, courage, and willingness to publish this first novel by a poet. And to Bruce Wagner for his early belief in and enthusiasm for *Vivienne*. Thanks to my friends and those with whom I've had great conversations about many of the topics at the core of this book: Stephanie Leone, Carter Tanton, Abraham Adams, Michelle Pellizzon Lipsitz, Abby Nocon, Emily Simon, John McFadden, Angie Speaks, Nina Power, Nick Jiorle, Vanessa Sinclair, Mary Wild, and Helen Rollins. I wrote this book during a rough year, and I thank those who stood by me.

NOTES

Artworks referenced in this book:

Hans Bellmer, *The Doll (La Poupée)*, 1936.
Hans Bellmer, *The Doll (Second Series)*, 1937-38.
Hans Bellmer, *The Machine-Gunneress in a State of Grace*, 1937.
Hans Bellmer, *The Red Embryo*, 1948.
Hans Bellmer, *Service Clos*, 1965.
Hans Bellmer, *Self-Portrait*, 1971.
Dorothea Tanning, *Eine Kleine Nachtmusik*, 1943.
Dorothea Tanning, *Tableau Vivant*, 1954.
Lee Miller, *Revenge on Culture*, 1940.
The Passion of Anna, directed by Ingmar Bergman, 1969.

Lars quotes from the Classics of Western Spirituality Edition version of Marguerite Porete's *The Mirror of Simple Souls* (c. 1300), translated by Ellen Babinsky.

When talking about venial sins, Vivienne quotes from the *Catechism of the Catholic Church*.

Velour quotes Ingeborg Bachmann ("I am writing with my burnt hand about the nature of fire.") who in turn was quoting Flaubert. Velour also references André Breton's *Nadja* (1928): "Beauty will be convulsive or will not be at all."

One of the commenters references something Simone Weil said in *The Need for Roots* (1949): "The destruction of the past is perhaps the greatest of all crimes." Another references a quote from Weil's *Gravity and Grace* (1952): "To love truth means to endure the void and, as a result, to accept death. Truth is on the side of death." Another quotes Erykah Badu: "Art is the absence of fear."

When talking about the clothing the characters are wearing, I was under the influence of and sometimes directly describing pieces by Martin Margiela, Ann Demeulemeester, Elena Velez, and Rick Owens.

The epigraph at the start of this book is lifted from *Hegel's Theory of Madness* (1995) by Daniel Berthold-Bond.

Although she is not mentioned directly, the life and work of Unica Zürn influenced *Vivienne* immensely: her relationship with Hans Bellmer, her death, her book *Dark Spring*, and her drawings from the 1960s.